You're About to Become a

Privileged Woman.

INTRODUCING
PAGES & PRIVILEGES™.

It's our way of thanking you for buying
our books at your favorite retail store.

GET ALL THIS FREE
WITH JUST ONE PROOF OF PURCHASE:

◆ Hotel Discounts up to 60% at home and abroad

◆ Travel Service - Guaranteed lowest published
   airfares plus 5% cash back on tickets

◆ $25 Travel Voucher

◆ Sensuous Petite Parfumerie collection ($50 value)

◆ Insider Tips Letter with sneak previews of
   upcoming books

◆ Mystery Gift (if you enroll before 6/15/95)

*You'll get a FREE personal card, too.
It's your passport to all these benefits– and to
even more great gifts & benefits to come!*

There's no club to join. No purchase commitment. No obligation.

As a *Privileged Woman,* you'll be entitled to all these *Free Benefits.* And *Free Gifts,* too.

To thank you for buying our books, we've designed an exclusive FREE program called *PAGES & PRIVILEGES™.* You can enroll with just one Proof of Purchase, and get the kind of luxuries that, until now, you could only read about.

*B*IG HOTEL DISCOUNTS

A privileged woman stays in the finest hotels. And so can you—at up to 60% off! Imagine standing in a hotel check-in line and watching as the guest in front of you pays $150 for the same room that's only costing you $60. Your *Pages & Privileges* discounts are good at Sheraton, Marriott, Best Western, Hyatt and thousands of other fine hotels all over the U.S., Canada and Europe.

*F*REE DISCOUNT TRAVEL SERVICE

A privileged woman is always jetting to romantic places. When <u>you</u> fly, just make one phone call for the lowest published airfare at time of booking—<u>or double the difference back!</u> PLUS—

you'll get a $25 voucher to use the first time you book a flight AND <u>5% cash back on every ticket you buy thereafter through the travel service!</u>

*F*REE GIFTS!

A privileged woman is always getting wonderful gifts.
Luxuriate in rich fragrances that will stir your senses (and his). This gift-boxed assortment of fine perfumes includes three popular scents, each in a beautiful designer bottle. <u>Truly Lace</u>...This luxurious fragrance unveils your sensuous side. <u>L'Effleur</u>...discover the romance of the Victorian era with this soft floral. <u>Muguet des bois</u>...a single note floral of singular beauty. This $50 value is yours—FREE when you enroll in *Pages & Privileges*! And it's just the beginning of the gifts and benefits that will be coming your way!

$50 VALUE

*F*REE INSIDER TIPS LETTER

A privileged woman is always informed. And you'll be, too, with our free letter full of fascinating information and sneak previews of upcoming books.

*M*ORE GREAT GIFTS & BENEFITS TO COME

A privileged woman always has a lot to look forward to.
And so will you. You get all these wonderful FREE gifts and benefits now with only one purchase...and there are no additional purchases required. However, each additional retail purchase of Harlequin and Silhouette books brings you a step closer to even more great FREE benefits like half-price movie tickets...and even more FREE gifts like these beautiful fragrance gift baskets:

L'Effleur...This basketful of romance lets you discover L'Effleur from head to toe, heart to home.

Truly Lace...A basket spun with the sensuous luxuries of Truly Lace, including Dusting Powder in a reusable satin and lace covered box.

*E*NROLL *N*OW!
Complete the Enrollment Form on the back of this card and become a Privileged Woman today!

Enroll Today in *PAGES & PRIVILEGES*™, the program that gives you Great Gifts and Benefits with just one purchase!

Enrollment Form

☐ *Yes!* I WANT TO BE A *PRIVILEGED WOMAN*.

Enclosed is one *PAGES & PRIVILEGES*™ Proof of Purchase from any Harlequin or Silhouette book currently for sale in stores (Proofs of Purchase are found on the back pages of books) and the store cash register receipt. Please enroll me in *PAGES & PRIVILEGES*™. Send my Welcome Kit and FREE Gifts -- and activate my FREE benefits -- immediately.

NAME (please print)

ADDRESS   APT. NO

CITY   STATE   ZIP/POSTAL CODE

PROOF OF PURCHASE

SAMPLE ONLY

Please allow 6-8 weeks for delivery. Quantities are limited. We reserve the right to substitute items. Enroll before October 31, 1995 and receive one full year of benefits.

**NO CLUB!
NO COMMITMENT!**
*Just one purchase brings you great **Free Gifts** and **Benefits!***
(See inside for details.)

Name of store where this book was purchased_____

Date of purchase_____

Type of store:

☐ Bookstore   ☐ Supermarket   ☐ Drugstore

☐ Dept. or discount store (e.g. K-Mart or Walmart)

☐ Other (specify)_____

Which Harlequin or Silhouette series do you usually read?

_____

Complete and mail with one Proof of Purchase and store receipt to:

U.S.: *PAGES & PRIVILEGES*™, P.O. Box 1960, Danbury, CT 06813-1960

Canada: *PAGES & PRIVILEGES*™, 49-6A The Donway West, P.O. 813, North York, ON M3C 2E8   PRINTED IN U.S.A

Dear Reader,

I have to admit, when I first met Kelly McGrath, I was ready to kill. Protecting a daughter is sheer instinct for a father, and all I wanted to do was throttle the teenage Adonis who had gotten Sandy into trouble. Something had to be done about Jarod and his parents. Or parent, as I quickly discovered!

Of course, I wasn't expecting a tiny blond whirlwind who hardly seemed capable of producing a six-foot-something, muscle-bound ball player. I must have scared the hell out of her that first day. But I quickly discovered Kelly could hold her own—and in Jarod's defense, she could fight just like a mountain lioness.

But the kids were in trouble together, and the two of us just had to swallow down our differences to help. For Kelly it was harder, since history seemed to be repeating itself. Then it got all kinds of complicated, because it wasn't quite so easy to condemn young Jarod when I began discovering myself that there was a woman I wanted beyond all thought and care and responsibility—his mother.

Dan Marquette

West Virginia

HEATHER GRAHAM POZZESSERE
All in the Family

West Virginia

Silhouette Books®

Published by Silhouette Books New York

America's Publisher of Contemporary Romance

To Anita and Dusty.
Many thanks for a wonderful time at
Harpers Ferry.

SILHOUETTE BOOKS
300 East 42nd St., New York, N.Y. 10017

ALL IN THE FAMILY

Copyright © 1987 by Heather Graham Pozzessere

ISBN: 0-373-45198-9

Published Silhouette Books 1987, 1993, 1995

All the characters in this book have no existence outside the imagination of the author and have no relation whatsoever to anyone bearing the same name or names. They are not even distantly inspired by any individual known or unknown to the author, and all incidents are pure invention.

® and ™ are trademarks used under license. Trademarks recorded with ® are registered in the United States Patent and Trademark Office, the Canadian Trade Marks Office and in other countries.

Printed in the U.S.A.

Prologue

She had been watching him for a long time when she finally came to the fence that day. Well, maybe not so long in days—she had only been in Bolivar for a month—but it felt like forever. She'd seen him first in the hallway, walking with his friends. She'd noticed his hair, like a beacon. It wasn't just blond, it was nearly white, and one lock slashed across the tan of his forehead like a beautiful ribbon of silk. And his eyes, blue, bright blue like the sky, were as startling and arresting as that hair.

Not that she could have missed him anyway. He was about six-foot-two—a standout in any crowd. Tall, blond and beautiful. He should have been a California beachboy, not a West Virginia mountain man.

Yet it had been his smile that had really drawn her. It had seemed like the epitome of romance to her young heart, straight out of a novel, sensual, fascinating. They had seen each other on her very first day, across the crowded hallway. Their eyes had met, and the world had stopped. Suddenly there was no one else, no one who mattered. She heard the beat of her own heart, and nothing else....

And then he had smiled.

It seemed as if she had been there forever, returning his gaze, unable to smile herself. Unable to even blush.

Then someone had tapped him on the shoulder and he had turned, and she had been released. But not really. The spell he had cast had stayed with her, and at every opportunity she had watched him, and now she was watching him again, her fingers curled around the wire fencing, tense and taut, her eyes trained on his tall form. He was wearing a helmet, shoulder pads and ridiculously tight pants; there were black marks beneath his eyes to ward off the sun's reflection, and he was filthy from numerous falls to the spring-wet earth. But he was still the most beautiful human being she had ever seen, and she smiled, because she knew he was aware that she was there, watching him. The new kid in town. She was patient; she could wait. She knew that he would come to her. She had known it that day in the hallway when their eyes had met so romantically, when the world had stood still, when there had been no one on earth except for the two of them.

A whistle shrilled, and the boys went running off the field. One of the coaches yelled at someone, and soon the field was nearly empty.

He remained. He tossed the football up in the air, caught it, tossed it again, caught it again. And then he stared at her and slowly smiled, and at last he walked toward her.

He reached the fence, and they stood just inches apart, only the wire separating them.

It happened again. The sky was gone; the earth was gone. Noise faded, and they were alone; they were all that mattered in the entire world. Silence seemed to reign, but it was an eloquent silence.

She was in love. Head over heels in love, and she would never love again as she did at the moment. They watched each other with all their feelings in their eyes.

"You're Sandy Marquette," he said at last.

"You know my name."

He smiled. A slow, rueful smile that was totally endearing.

"I know everything about you. You've just moved here from D.C., and your birthday is the second of September, and your father is some kind of historian and..."

His voice trailed away for just a moment. Then that smile touched his face again, more wistful than before. "You're the most beautiful girl I've ever seen. You must be here to break the hearts of all us poor mountain boys."

She laughed, a husky sound that caught in her throat. Warmth raced through her, and she felt breathless, barely able to speak.

"I'd take a mountain man anytime."

It wasn't meant to be sexy; she was just being honest. She barely knew him—all she knew were those looks that had passed between them—but those exchanges were as good as vows; they were promises to last a lifetime.

"This mountain man?" he inquired softly.

"No other. Ever," she whispered.

The spring breeze picked up, touching them both. A shadow rich with dark warmth and promise fell over the valley. He dropped the football, and his fingers curled over hers where they clung to the fencing. Just touching.

"I've got to shower," he finally told her.

"I'll wait."

It was some time before he could release her, but at last he did. He stared at her as he walked across the field. When he tripped, she laughed, and so did he. He waved and forced himself to turn around. To hurry, hurry so that he could get back to her. Even so, he dropped the soap a dozen times. His fingers were shaking so badly that he had to shove his hands into his pockets and whistle when he finally left the locker room. Then he walked back to meet her at the fence, and they smiled again, both aware that he would have to walk around to meet her without that obstacle between them.

She was sophisticated, he told himself. She was superior to anything that had ever touched his life before. He couldn't behave like a bumpkin!

Hold something back, she warned herself. He was the most popular guy in school, adored by everyone. He was beautiful, he was like a god, and she was just the new girl, and she had to be careful....

He came around to her and paused awkwardly. Then that slow smile lit his face again, and he held out his hand toward her. He watched her eyes as their fingers intertwined.

"Want—want to get—" He had to clear his throat. "A soda or—"

"I don't care. I don't care what we do."

"We could drive—" he began, but then his face fell, and he laughed. "Except that I don't have a car. I came with Pete, but then I took one look at you and forgot everything."

"I have mine," she said.

She led him to the parking lot and to her brand-new, little red sports car.

He groaned inwardly, feeling all the differences between them more keenly.

She was a rich girl, and he . . .

"Yours? I mean, your own?" he asked hesitantly.

She nodded and handed him the keys. He took them and paused, and then he saw all the wistfulness and magic in her eyes. He realized that nothing on heaven or earth mattered except for the two of them.

He opened the door for her, then came around to the driver's seat.

He loved the car. He loved the subtle scent of her perfume. He loved the girl who was sitting beside him.

He drove to a quiet place by the river and parked. They talked, and finally darkness fell.

He talked about the river and told her about rafting and swimming, and he told her about the cabin up in the mountains by the stream. He told her about the deer that would come and eat right out of your hand, and about how when a fire crackled in the hearth and night descended, there was no better place to be. She tried to tell him about her life, but she couldn't think of much to say, because it felt as if her life had begun with her first glimpse of him, and that nothing before him mattered.

She would never have thought of the time; he was the one who worried. She would have dropped him off at his house, but he wouldn't hear of it.

He would always see her safely home, he promised.

And besides, he needed to walk. Needed to feel the air and the earth and savor the feeling, the feeling of knowing her, of loving her.

He began to dream of her, awake and asleep. He'd had a 4.0 average for all of his high school years, but now everything he read turned to gibberish.

That, he knew, would have to change. Smiling by the light of his desk lamp, he chewed his eraser and thought about the situation. He had to maintain that 4.0. Now, more than ever, he had to go through with all his plans.

He was going to marry her. As soon as possible.

He told her so the next day. At first she was stunned, but then she hugged him. Then the bell began to ring for class, so he whispered that they would talk later, that as soon as school was out they would head for that cabin, where they could be alone to plan their future.

That afternoon, while it was still light, they wandered to the stream. They wound up laughing and showering each other with the cold mountain water. Naturally he built a fire to warm them up.

By its gentle light they gazed into each other's eyes, and then he touched her, and then . . .

Love led the way for her, a gentle, tender path to an ecstasy that was both sweet and torrid.

She'd known she belonged to him, since their eyes had met across the hall, but now she felt as if he would be a part of her forever and ever. They would marry, yet marriage could be only a legal sanction of what they had already shared.

Others might talk and call them foolish, say they were young, that they knew nothing. That they had so much to learn, so many paths to follow. At their ages it was a crush, only puppy love.

Puppy love...

No one had ever loved so deeply, she knew. And no one had ever made love as they had.

Love.

He was in love, he thought. They would get married as soon as possible, no matter what. Parental opposition, screaming, shouting, reproach—nothing would stop him, although he would be deeply sorry if his mother didn't understand.

But not even that could be allowed to matter....

He would give up anything. That was it. This was love. She was his life.

He wanted to run out of the cabin, run out stark naked, and pound his fists against his chest, because she made him feel so male and strong and wonderful. He wanted to proclaim to the world that she was his, his forever.

But he knew that wasn't such a smart idea.

He turned to her, and, as if she could read his mind, she warned softly that they had to take care, had to move slowly, had to keep their love a very special secret.

They would meet whenever they could. They would cherish each other and every moment until they could be together forever.

Chapter 1

"Take that, you dastardly, devilish dragon!"

Kelly tried the words aloud, shrugged, grimaced, then added more pencil strokes to her paper, resting her feet on the rungs of her chair as she surveyed her morning's work.

Umm. Hard to judge. But this installment of the *Dark of the Moon* was due tomorrow, and she simply had to take care of the Fairy Queen and Daryl the Devilish Dragon by tonight.

"Easy," she murmured to herself. "Slay him. Off with his head!" But she couldn't do that, of course. *Dark of the Moon* was written for children, it took place in a fantasy land where mythical creatures learned lessons about life, teaching them to the children in the process. She couldn't go around lopping off her characters' heads.

"Okay, then, Daryl, what are you going to say here, huh?" she asked her character. Daryl—massive and muscular and mischievous—stared up at her with his big, slightly tilted eyes and defied his creator to reproach him.

She frowned slightly, wondering what was disturbing her, then realized that she really did have the capacity to tune out the world. The echo that was resounding in the air hinted that someone had been out on her front steps ringing her doorbell for quite some time.

"Jarod! Jarod, could you get the door, please?"

Kelly stared at Daryl again, knitting her brows and chewing her eraser. Come on, come on, Daryl, she coaxed him in silence. What are you going to say in return? Maybe I should have you cringe and cry; maybe I should have you lower those long eyelashes and beg forgiveness with such a wicked look beneath those lids that the kids will be ready for trouble next time.

The doorbell was still ringing. Kelly looked up in disgust. "Jarod!"

Was he even home? Maybe that was Jarod ringing the doorbell because he'd forgotten his key. He had become very forgetful lately—worse than she was.

"Oh, hell!"

Kelly tossed down her pencil and padded barefoot from her office to the hall and to the door. She should have looked through the peephole—Jarod was always warning her that she was too trusting—but she was annoyed at having been interrupted, so she merely threw the door open with a bang that threatened the old hinges.

"What—" she began, but her question, short as it was, never had a chance to be spoken.

"Where's your father? I want to see him now, young lady. Right now!"

Kelly felt fury settle over her as she stared up at the total stranger blocking her doorway. She was accustomed to staring up at a son who stood over six feet tall, so she had no trouble meeting his eyes, her own narrowing with instant hostility. Yet, despite that hostility, she fought the urge to step back a foot.

His hair was dark auburn, and it cut a slightly disheveled swath across his forehead, as if he had been brushing it back in agitation, but had finally gotten tired of fighting with it. He wasn't just tall; he was built as solidly as a wall, a fact made easy to notice by the snug fit of his worn jeans over his trim hips and long legs, and the way his navy knit shirt hugged his taut biceps and broad shoulders.

He had flashing dark eyes, a straight nose, and a square jaw. And he looked as furious as Kelly herself. People just don't act like this around here, she thought.

He might have been handsome if his features hadn't been so hard and angry. As it was, she couldn't escape the feeling that she really should step back. He was clearly dangerous. Jarod had been justified in warning her that she shouldn't open the door so readily, she realized.

"Where is your father!"

The words thundered out at her again, and she felt a rekindling of her initial fury. She didn't step back after all. Instead she straightened to the limits of her barefoot, five-foot-two frame and squared her shoulders, lifting her chin regally and staring at him with what she hoped was total and absolute amusement and scorn.

Just who the hell did he think he was, and what did he want?

"My father, sir, is in Vancouver—I believe. I don't keep a schedule of his whereabouts."

The stranger paused slightly, gazing down at her with his dark brows knit together. He really was a very good-looking man, Kelly thought, her heart skipping slightly. Then she reminded herself that he was also rude and abrasive, and she set her hands on her hips, casting a glance of restrained impatience his way.

"Get me your mother then. Now—please."

A sigh of irritation escaped her, and she felt her own temper rise to the boiling point as he brushed past her into the hallway of the old house, critically surveying everything in sight. He didn't go any farther, though, just watched her with annoyance, as if she were a child who was purposely and willfully attempting to delay him.

She stared at him with startled surprise, then smiled slowly—maliciously—in realization. He *did* think she was a child!

Kelly closed the door and leaned against it, crossing her arms over her chest—smiling as sweetly as she could. Her blond ponytail, bare feet and diminutive size had misled him, but that didn't mean she had to show him any mercy.

"Where is your mother, please?" he said again, sighing with exasperation.

She swallowed back a touch of sadness and replied with a definite bite, "Six feet under. Now just what is your problem?"

"What?" He was definitely startled.

Kelly set her jaw grimly. "Deceased. My mother is deceased. Now, since you've barged into my home—"

"You live here alone?" he demanded.

"Not exactly. I live with my son."

"You're his mother?"

He spoke with such absolute astonishment that Kelly paused, touched by the irony of the situation. "If being 'his' mother means that I'm the mother of Jarod McGraw, then yes. Now—"

"You can't be!"

"But I am."

His eyes raked over her—so totally and assessingly that she longed to slap him.

"If you can't—"

"Where's your husband?"

Kelly gritted her teeth, wishing desperately that she had the size and strength to pick the man up by his collar and deliver him back to the step on the seat of his pants. Her eyes narrowed even further, and she said, "Also deceased, I'm afraid. So, since you've barged your way so rudely into my house, I suggest you tell me your business as quickly as possible. Otherwise I'll feel obliged to ask the police to rid me of your obnoxious presence."

He didn't scare easily. But then, he didn't smile, either, only continued to stare at her grimly. "I've been considering the possibility of calling in the police myself, Mrs. McGraw. Somehow I had this ardent hope that I could come over here and in some miraculous way discover that it couldn't be true. But it *is* true—I can see that right now. You must have been a true child bride, lady. And it's more than obvious that you don't have a bit of control over that overgrown, irresponsible Adonis you've raised!''

What? Now he was really in trouble! He could hold any opinion of her that he chose, but any intelligent man should have more sense than to insult a woman's only child!

And especially Jarod, she thought with a pang. Jarod; bright, considerate—exceptionally sensitive. In almost eighteen years, she had never come across anyone who didn't like Jarod!

Somehow she kept a smile on her face. She cocked her head pleasantly, then moved away from the door. "Excuse me, will you? I still don't know who the hell you are, but I think that I *will* call in the police."

His eyes flashed, and Kelly was torn between panic—he was barely in control, truly enraged!—and total indignation.

He wasn't from the area. None of the locals would behave this way. Barging in, making demands. The man wasn't even remotely civilized.

"Please, do call them," he drawled, crossing his arms over his chest, leaning comfortably against her staircase.

"I'm going to—right now," Kelly said warningly.

He nodded as she started past him.

"I really don't know that much about the law," he said evenly. "The charge might be statutory rape."

"What?"

Kelly stopped dead in astonishment, then spun around to face the man. She wondered whether this was some hideous joke. She couldn't believe any of this. It was all a fantasy.

Just like her world in *Dark of the Moon*, where nothing terrible was ever real.

But he was real. This stranger. Straightening now, no longer so comfortable against the wall. Tall and large and dangerously filling the peaceful sanctity of her world with his ominous presence.

"What—what are you talking about?" Kelly asked slowly.

"Rape, Mrs. McGraw. Statutory. Your son Jarod."

She shook her head, furiously denying his words. She stepped a few feet backward. Shock had made her defensive.

Then her initial amazement at his accusation faded, and she stood her ground. He was insane, she thought, beginning to smile. He had the wrong boy. He didn't know Jarod, couldn't know Jarod. It was that simple. Serious, astute, charming, responsible Jarod. The kid with both academic and athletic scholarship offers coming in from the best schools in the country. A son in whom no parent could ever find a greater source of pride...

"You don't take this seriously, Mrs. McGraw? Maybe I should have put the call in to the sheriff's office first. Maybe I shouldn't have come over here. I meant to be calm and reasonable—"

"Calm and reasonable? You're a madman! And you don't know what you're talking about. Rape? Jarod? Never! I don't know who or what—"

"Who? My daughter, that's who, Mrs. McGraw. An innocent young girl with a good head on her shoulders until your overgrown barbarian of a half-back—"

"Jarod has more manners and style in his little finger than you'll ever have in your entire overgrown body, mister! Now if your little tart of a daughter waltzed by my son, offering herself—"

"Lady, don't you ever—" He reached her in a single stride, and his hands fell on her shoulders. She felt as if she were suddenly at the mercy of some maddened lunatic; Eric the Red, perhaps—or Satan himself.

Suddenly he seemed to realize that he was touching her, realize his anger, realize his potential for violence. He drew his hands back quickly and stared at them, apparently stunned by his own behavior. But he was still staring at her, and his look seemed every bit as menacing as his touch could ever be. He was like Daryl, her fire-breathing dragon. Kelly's heart beat painfully, and she could hear her breath rise and fall.

Perhaps we're both barbarians, she thought. Parents defending their offspring. She gave herself a little shake.

"Don't you ever—" she shouted back, and then she gasped for air to keep speaking. "Don't you ever come flaming in here like a torch again, attacking Jarod! You have no right. You can't—"

She broke off, a little dazed, as the front door flew open.

Jarod was there.

Beautiful, tall, blond Jarod, a frown furrowing his handsome brow, concern written all over his clean-cut features. He must have heard the shouting in the street. He had been frightened for her; he had obviously rushed in as quickly as possible.

"Mom?" He said the word as a question, staring at the strange visitor. A sense of relief flooded through Kelly. Jarod didn't know this man. The stranger was obviously mistaken—some wild outrage and grief had sent him here, but he was in the wrong place, after the wrong boy. His terrified daughter had apparently just thrown out some name....

"Jarod?" the stranger asked him.

Jarod nodded. And then Kelly began to feel ill, really ill. Something like recognition had entered her son's eyes, and he looked both anxious and wary.

"Sandy?" he gasped out, taking a step into the room. "She's—she's all right? She's not hurt or anything?"

Kelly inhaled sharply. "You know this man?" she demanded.

Jarod barely spared her a glance. He kept walking anxiously toward the man.

A redheaded lunatic. A man in such a frenzy that he seemed quite capable of violence...

She told herself that this delicate offspring she was trying to defend was six-foot-two and weighed in at about two hundred pounds. He was a football player, for heaven's sake.

It was just that this strange Eric the Red was even taller than her son—and broadened with the muscles of a man, while her son was still a boy in many ways.

No! she thought vehemently. There would be no fight. Not here.

"You're Mr. Marquette, her father, aren't you?" Jarod asked the stranger. "Nothing's happened, has it? There hasn't been an accident or anything, has there?"

Kelly was glad that he wasn't speaking to her, because she had suddenly become speechless. She could only stare from her son to the man, feeling the room spin.

Jarod had just made her a spectator, a spectator in her own home. To his life! When she had given so much of her own life to him, when she had prided herself on the depth of her communication with her teenage child.

Not a child.

She had never realized it until now. Jarod was not a child. He would be eighteen in a few months. He was almost a man.

She blinked quickly, staring at the stranger. At the man who Jarod didn't know—but recognized.

The man who was staring at Jarod. Marquette. Jarod had called him Marquette. It seemed like an eternity had passed since Jarod had spoken, but it had really been only seconds. And this Mr. Marquette seemed to have calmed down a bit at Jarod's appearance.

Maybe he realized that Jarod's concern was real and intense. That Jarod could never have hurt anyone, never attacked any girl. He just didn't have it in him. Oh, he wasn't that humble. He knew that he had magnetism. But he had never used it against anyone. In fact, he had always stood up for the weaker children. He always asked the wallflowers to dance, and he helped the weakest kids learn to get the basketball through the hoop.

"There hasn't been any accident," Marquette said with deceptive calm, watching Jarod carefully.

"Then ... ?"

"Jarod," Kelly interposed. "Do you know this man? Who is Sandy?"

Neither of them paid her the slightest heed. They kept staring at each other over her head.

"I demand to know—" she began, still bewildered, afraid to face the dawning truth.

She never finished. That dawning truth broke over her full force with Marquette's next words.

"Sandy is pregnant."

Jarod hadn't known that, Kelly realized. He stumbled slightly, turning white.

He looked broken. Well, he should, Kelly thought. He wasn't even eighteen yet. Every promise in the world lay open to him. Destroyed, if this was true. Destroyed. How well she knew.

She reeled under a new onslaught of fury. There was Marquette, standing like an avenging angel, so convinced of his little girl's innocence. Well, it couldn't be true! Jarod simply wasn't like that! Marquette's precious daughter might have been running around with the entire senior class; she might have chosen Jarod's name simply because he was every young girl's fantasy!

Kelly stepped forward and said scornfully, "Come on, Mr. Marquette. Perhaps we *should* call in the police. Or perhaps...perhaps you should take greater care with your accusations. The father is so often the last to know."

"Just what do you mean, Mrs. McGraw?" His eyes were narrowed again.

He was about to breathe fire, she was certain. But Kelly wasn't about to let Jarod take the rap if the man's daughter had been running around with every kid in town.

"What I'm saying, Mr. Marquette, is that it just might be possible that your daughter seduced not only my son, but half of the senior class. What I'm saying is that—"

Kelly wasn't sure quite what happened then. Marquette stiffened, the expression on his face explosive, and took a step forward. Jarod let out a gasp and came charging in. He swung at Marquette who ducked.

Jarod's fist—a powerful weapon—connected with his mother's jaw instead. Kelly felt the ringing pain; then she felt the world spin. Fury faded, and she slumped to the floor, seeing nothing but black.

Marquette reached for her, stooping quickly. Jarod fell to his knees beside his mother, still trying to defend her. He looked up quickly into Marquette's eyes.

They were Sandy's eyes, except that Sandy's were so much softer. This guy's were hard—like his frame.

"Don't touch her!" Jarod rasped out.

"Son, *you* hit her," the older man said in an ironic tone.

Marquette seemed to have lost a lot of his anger. He ignored Jarod and reached beneath Kelly's shoulders. Jarod reached for her, too.

"She's my mother!"

Marquette actually laughed. "Take her, then. It won't do any good for the two of us to sit here fighting over her unconscious body!"

Unbelievably, Jarod found himself grinning as he lifted Kelly.

"Why did you fly at me?" Marquette demanded.

"I thought you were going to—to—"

"To hurt her? Your mother?"

"Well, she was talking about your daughter. She doesn't know Sandy, sir. If she did . . ." Jarod's voice trailed away. "Well, you see, Mom is small, but she's a fighter." He paused, swallowing again. "You know how you feel about Sandy. Well, Mom feels the same way about me, I suppose."

Marquette nodded, studying Jarod. It was impossible not to like the boy. It wasn't just looks—Sandy would never have been swayed by looks alone—it was the honesty about him. It was something about those eyes, about his clear stare, that promised integrity.

You should have thought this one out first, Marquette! he warned himself, too late. He just hadn't been able to help himself. Sandy was all the beauty in his life; she was his pride, his joy. Somehow he had never realized that she had grown up. He had always thought of her as his little girl, as pure as a white lily, and some primal instinct had told him that she had been taken, attacked or seduced, that she couldn't be to blame.

Even if no one was to blame, he felt ill. She was so young! A baby about to have a baby! There were alternatives, of course. There were a host of things that could be done.

What had to be done was the right thing, of course. And they had to have help, these two. They were so young....

Jarod was still standing there, holding his mother. Dan Marquette frowned suddenly. "My God, she's tiny. I thought at first that she was your sister."

Jarod laughed, a little proudly. "She's always been the best-looking mom in town!" he said. Then he realized that they were both just standing there. Sandy's father—and him. He-who-had-just-struck-his-own-mother!

"I'll, uh, carry her to the couch," he said, ashamed of not having thought of that right away.

"I'll get some ice. Where's the kitchen?"

Jarod indicated the far side of the house. Then he lifted his mother and headed into the den. Bookshelves lined the walls, and the warm, golden oak furniture ranged from a desk at one end to an entertainment center at the other. He laid his mother on an afghan-covered couch close to the television. If she'd been conscious she could have looked out the window to the lawn and the street beyond.

He stared down at his mother worriedly. She was very pale, except for a place on her chin where a dark bruise was already forming.

"Oh, Mom!" Jarod whispered miserably. Pregnant. Sandy was pregnant. They hadn't been very careful. Yes, they had—after the first time. You only needed one time. Pregnant. With his child.

Jarod's fingers trembled as he smoothed the blond hair from his mother's forehead. He was going to be a father. He and Sandy were going to be parents. The responsibility of it was overwhelming, but at the same time he felt a wonderful, mystical beauty and pride. They were going to have a baby. Sandy, his Sandy, was carrying his child.

His mother was going to be so disappointed. And Sandy's father was—well, enraged.

But they had to understand. He and Sandy loved each other.

Marquette came in, carrying ice wrapped in a cloth and a bottle of Kelly's best brandy.

Jarod gazed at him anxiously. "You think she's all right, don't you? Maybe I should call a doctor."

Marquette didn't look at him as he knelt beside the couch, his dark eyes intent upon Kelly McGraw. He frowned slightly and shook his head. "No, you just nicked her. She'll be fine." He set the ice down, but held on to the brandy. "You have any ammonia or smelling salts around?" he asked Jarod.

Jarod shook his head and lifted his hands lamely. "No one here runs around passing out. Usually."

Marquette nodded and poured out a small shot of brandy. He lifted Kelly's head and forced a little brandy between her lips. She coughed, and some of the liquor trailed down her cheek. Her eyes fluttered, and Marquette set the brandy down, satisfied.

Jarod stared at him over his mother's form. "Mr. Marquette . . ."

He glanced up, and Jarod studied his face. There was a lot of him in Sandy, yet he was as masculine as a man could get, while Sandy . . .

There had never been anyone more feminine, more beautiful. Where her father's features were hard, Sandy's were fine. Those dark eyes, with the spark of fire and life in them, those were the same. He would have recognized Marquette anywhere.

The man no longer seemed angry, just resigned, disappointed. He wanted to hate me, Jarod thought. But he doesn't. And that made it all the more imperative that he explain.

"I love her, sir. I love Sandy with all my heart. We intended to marry each other . . . anyway." He lowered his eyes when he finished speaking.

Marquette studied him for a moment. "Jarod, you and Sandy have to take time. You have to look at all the options. Hand me that ice, will you?"

Jarod guiltily remembered his mother and passed over the ice. Marquette pressed it against Kelly's chin. She blinked again, and tried to sit up.

It wasn't a nightmare. That was her first thought. She had wanted to awaken and find that it had been a dream. That this red-haired, fire-breathing monster had been a figment of her imagination, created because she was so desperate to get her work done.

But it was all real, Kelly acknowledged instantly. The fire-breathing monster was still here—holding ice against her chin. She was stretched out on the couch, and he was kneeling over her. Jarod was there, too, staring down at her. And her chin hurt like blue blazes.

Jarod had struck her. Of course, he hadn't been trying to. He'd been aiming for Marquette. And Marquette...

Her eyes flew open wide with alarm, her heart thundering painfully, and then she relaxed, feeling a little bit ridiculous. Obviously Marquette hadn't taken up the fight. Jarod looked just fine. They were both there, calm, rational, staring at her.

"Oh, God," she breathed, and closed her eyes again. A hand fell on her forehead. Marquette's. Long-fingered, yet light. Massive. She swallowed sharply and swung her feet to the ground, rejecting his concerned touch with a wave.

"I'm all right—"

But she broke off because her head was spinning. Not just with pain, but with the truth that was growing more evident and undeniable every second. Jarod had gotten this man's daughter pregnant. Jarod wasn't denying anything. Jarod was concerned. Jarod was...

For a moment her mind went blank. Then it whipped into action again. There were options. All kinds of options. They had to do what was best for all of them. No, she acknowledged honestly, not all of them. The two of them. Jarod and—what was her name? Sandy.

Sandy! Damn you, Sandy! she thought vehemently. How could you? Why didn't you...?

But that wasn't fair, and she knew it. She of all people should know it. Jarod was every bit as responsible as the girl, and he was going to behave responsibly now.

"Here."

She tried to blink and open her eyes again. Marquette was stuffing something into her hand. He was still staring at her, silent but concerned.

"Are you all right?" he asked quietly as she wrapped her fingers around the brandy glass.

"No, not at all," she murmured, grinning dryly. "But my jaw isn't broken or anything."

He stood. She wished he hadn't. She liked dealing with him much better when he was on his knees.

"I'm sorry, Mrs. McGraw," he said suddenly. She stared at him, a bit incredulous at his change.

But he hadn't really changed, she thought. He was as hard as ever, as determined. Just more polite.

"I shouldn't have come over this way. I acted without thinking. Maybe you can understand what I felt when I first talked to my daughter. Maybe...you can't. I'm afraid I reacted out of pure anger. I wanted to be reasonable, and I wasn't."

Kelly lowered her head, wishing for a moment that they had remained on the battleground, because now she was forced to admit that she had replied in kind. She had all but called his daughter a little whore, and really, she didn't normally behave that way, either. Then again, when one was attacked...

"If you're all right, I'll leave you. I'll call, to see when we can discuss this situation."

To Kelly's amazement, Marquette turned and strode from the room.

Suddenly Jarod stood. "Mr. Marquette! Wait, please!"

The man was already out the front door, but Kelly saw him pause on the walkway. Jarod saw him, too, and started to follow.

"Jarod!" Kelly called.

He looked back at her, and sorrow flashed through his eyes. He started to walk away, then came back. He leaned down and kissed her forehead, looking at her anxiously, but then he stood.

"Are you okay, Mom? I'm sorry. I've never been so sorry about anything in my entire life. Honest to God. But I've got to go. I have to see her. I have to see Sandy. She's—she's pregnant. She's going to have my baby. I have to see her. Can you understand?"

He kissed her forehead again, then started for the door to catch up with Marquette.

"Jarod, wait! This is serious! We have to talk. We have to—"

"Mother, please! I just have to see that Sandy is all right! I'll be back, I promise, and then we'll talk."

The door banged. Kelly was on her feet, her fury aimed at her only child, but standing made her dizzy, and she had to drop back to the couch. She could see them through the window, though: her tall, handsome son, and the even taller red-haired man. Leaving together.

"Jarod, I'll...I'll clobber you for this!" she swore. But of course she wouldn't clobber him. She'd never clobbered him. And he'd been way too big for ages, anyway.

She poured herself more brandy and gulped it down.

"Oh, Jarod!" she whispered. She stood again, and began pacing the room, still half in shock. She tried to retrace everything that had happened. Marquette bursting in like a maddened lunatic with his accusations...

Accusations that were in part true. She'd heard it straight from Jarod's own lips.

Kelly finished off the brandy as she continued to pace. She barely noticed the dull ache in her jaw.

Jarod—and Marquette! Standing up at the end and acting so damn noble. Sorry, I'll call you. Then walking out, after everything he had caused.

Kelly moved to the couch, poured another brandy and sank back on the cushions. She stared blankly out the windows.

"Jarod. Jarod, Jarod, Jarod."

And then she started to think about Marquette again.

She threw her glass across the room into the fireplace, gritting her teeth at the sound of the shattering glass.

"Damn you, Jarod! If you had to get a girl pregnant, couldn't you have picked one with a different father?"

Then she started to laugh, because the thought was so ridiculous. And then, all alone, she started to cry.

Because it was just like history repeating itself, and she didn't know if she sympathized more with her own son—or with the girl she had never seen.

Chapter 2

Kelly remained on the couch, stunned, for several minutes. Then she remembered that in the midst of this tempest they had both seen fit to walk out on her. Even her own son, after half crushing her jaw, had gone running out.

That made her mad. She forgot about her pain and began to storm around the house ranting. That lasted awhile, and then she thought again of the seriousness of the whole thing and burst into fresh tears.

In the end, she returned to her drawings. She turned Daryl the Devilish Dragon into a new type of monster—one with Marquette's face—and she let Esmeralda, the Fairy Queen, chase him around with a fat wooden spoon, catch him, tie him up and clobber him.

Of course, she really needed to get some *real* work done. And letting Esmeralda behave so violently would never do. But it had felt awfully good for the moment.

"Work!" she murmured aloud disgustedly. Who the hell could work when she had just discovered that her teenage son was about to get slapped with a paternity suit?

She threw down her pencil and went to the den, her temper flaring anew at the thought that she had watched them both go, just like a bump on a log. She didn't even have the faintest idea of what Sandy Marquette was like. What she looked like, how she sounded—Kelly didn't know anything about the girl at all.

She pressed her lips together grimly and picked up the phone book with determination. But no Marquette was listed. She tried information for his phone number and address, but the operator was unable to help her. Her anger against him grew. Who did he think he was, demanding an unlisted number?

But just when she thought she would scream and run out into the street and start going door to door, the front door opened and Jarod came into the house.

He looked dazed. Starry-eyed. He was even smiling. Not a big, wide smile. A dizzy type of smile. He was completely gone over this girl who had just destroyed his life. Kelly wanted to slap him, wanted to slap that silly grin off his face.

She set her hands on her hips and stared at him coolly. But before she could talk, he came closer and knelt before her, taking her hand in a manner so touching that all her anger escaped and she felt again the deep chill of sorrow.

"Mom, I *am* sorry, very sorry, for the way I've disappointed you," he said softly.

She jerked her hand away. She couldn't be soft—not now. Not when he was behaving like such a fool.

"Jarod, really, get off the ground, please!" He did, and she discovered herself growing annoyed all over again. He didn't seem to realize what he had done at all. He was sorry, but not for the deed, or even for its repercussions. He was only sorry because she was upset.

"Jarod—" she began. She turned away from him and lowered her head, suddenly acutely tired. "Jarod . . . don't you understand? Don't you see what you've done?"

It took him a long while to answer.

"I love her, Mom," he finally said softly. She didn't say anything, and he hesitated again. He didn't fidget, though; he didn't even seem uncomfortable. He was just standing his ground. Not a boy, very much a man.

"Mom, you don't know her. You have no right to judge her."

"I'm not judging her! If she were as saintly as Joan of Arc, you'd still be in the middle of a disaster!"

"A child isn't a disaster, Mother."

Great. All she needed was Jarod preaching to her—and sounding ridiculously wise.

"Jarod, you're not thinking. I know a child isn't a disaster. It *is* a tremendous responsibility. A baby makes a new ball game out of driving to the store for milk. A baby is constant, Jarod. It won't wait, unattended, while you go to school, to football practice, to a concert with your friends. Then there are the hospital costs, the pediatrician, the diapers—"

"Mom, I know all that!"

"And?" She turned around, one brow arched.

"I'll deal with it."

"You're not even out of high school!"

Kelly didn't want to scream; she really didn't want to get hysterical. She didn't want to alienate him—she wanted to help him. But he was being so blasé!

He returned her stare evenly. "When the baby is born, I'll be out of high school."

She swallowed sharply. "College lies ahead of you, Jarod. Four years of it."

He shrugged. "If I have to wait, I will."

"What will you do in the meantime?"

"Get a job."

"Doing what? *Doing what?*" Her voice was rising again. She tried to lower it; she was going to cry again. "Cook at a hamburger joint? That will barely cover the hospital costs if you work nine to five for months!"

His jaw tightened. Kelly lowered her eyes, biting her lip. He knew it. He knew everything that she was going to say—and he would stand his ground.

"Oh, Jarod. And what about Sandy? Think about her for a moment. At a ridiculously young age she's going to be saddled with an infant. Suppose she's home with the child while you're off frying hamburgers? What if they won't let her finish high school? What about college for her? What about her dreams? What about—"

"Do you want Sandy to get an abortion?" Jarod broke in coolly. Very coolly.

She winced, closing her eyes, gritting her teeth. No, she didn't want that. She didn't exactly know why, but she couldn't bear the thought. Still, this wasn't her life they were discussing. It was Jarod's life, and Sandy's.

"Mother?" he pressed softly.

"Don't, Jarod. Don't push me. I'm not saying that. Besides, what I want doesn't matter. What's best for the both of you is what matters." She hesitated, for just the slightest second. "Jarod, you're sure? You're absolutely sure that Sandy is pregnant, and you're sure that—that it's yours?"

"Yes!"

"I'm not attacking her, Jarod," Kelly told him wearily. "I don't even know the girl."

She started to laugh, then. Laugh and feel so weak that she had to sink into a chair.

"I don't even know her! You've had this great affair going on for who knows how long now, and I've never even met the girl!"

"Mom—"

Jarod looked uncomfortable at last. He folded his hands, unfolded them helplessly, folded them again. He looked around, distressed, while she laughed. "Mom," he said worriedly, "want a drink? Some tea. Maybe I should make some tea."

She waved a hand at him. She was still laughing, yet tears were squeezing out of her eyes. "Oh, Jarod!" We've talked...you and I! I always thought we had such good discussions. I knew you were going to grow up, that you'd eventually become involved. I just—I thought I'd taught you to be smart!"

He flushed, suddenly looking like a boy again—in contrast to the man he was fast becoming. Damn, Kelly realized, watching him. He'd gotten so old! When, how, had she missed it? He'd outsized her for years, but now everything about him seemed so much—older. More mature. His face, the way he stood, the way he moved. She felt ancient.

He sighed, and they stared at each other. "We were smart. Just not—not the first time."

"Oh," she said simply.

"I never meant to seduce her."

"Maybe that's because she seduced you."

He didn't answer that—though he probably longed to do so! But she was his mother, and even in his state of blissful infatuation he seemed to remember that.

And she was taking unfair shots. Sarcastic shots. She owed him more than that. She'd kept their relationship strong for all these years by being honest, by being fair. Since he'd been a little boy, she'd always been careful to listen to him, really listen. She always tried to explain when she said no.

Most of the time, anyway. She was human, and she'd also said "Because I said no, that's why!" But not often.

She lifted her hands weakly and shook her head, giving him a rueful smile. "I'm still in shock, Jarod. I'm not thinking very well. You know—" She hesitated, biting her lip. "You know that I'm going to help you, whatever you decide, in any way that I can. We've just got to—well, we've got to really discuss it."

"Mom . . ."

His voice was very soft, and he was on his knees again, beside her chair, and they were hugging each other. She found that she was crying again, smoothing back his beautiful blond hair. "I just had such dreams for you! And maybe that wasn't fair. I can't dream your dreams for you—that's your own right. But, oh, Jarod, the opportunities that were opening for you! Maybe they'll still be there, maybe it can work out, maybe . . ."

Her voice trailed away. Maybe. Oh, God, he just didn't see it! College alone was such a horrible expense, even with a scholarship. And now a baby, too....

Jarod looked up at her, taking both of her hands in his. "I love you," he told her. "I didn't want to leave you, but had to. I had to see Sandy. The way her father came in...well, I had to tell her that she wasn't alone. That I really loved her. That I've never cop out on her."

Kelly nodded feebly.

"It's going to be okay."

She laughed. "I'm the parent. I think I'm supposed to be saying that to you, except that—" She cut herself off sharply. He'd find out soon enough if they went through with a marriage and the birth of their child. They'd find out how hard it was to have an infant and nothing else in the world, to be scratching for change just to get to eat out once in a while.

He didn't say anything to her; he just squeezed her hands and stood up. "I wish I could say something to help."

"I wish *I* could," she told him quietly.

He grinned suddenly. "You might be a grandmother before your thirty-sixth birthday. The town will really talk!"

Kelly cast him a warning glare. "That didn't help one bit, Jarod, and I'll thank you not to tell me that again!"

He laughed, but she didn't dare. She'd get hysterical again. She shook her head, trying to clear it. "Really, we've just scratched the surface here. There's so much that you have to think about, and honestly,

Jarod, you're not being fair if you don't give Sandy a chance to consider the options, too. We've—''

"We're going to talk. All of us, okay?"

"All of us?" Kelly frowned.

"Sandy—oh, wait till you meet her. She's wonderful! Me, you, Mr. Marquette."

"What about Sandy's mother?"

"She doesn't have one."

"Everyone has a mother. Are they divorced, or is she dead?"

"I don't know. I just know that she doesn't have a mother right now. Just her father. And he's asked me and you over for dinner tomorrow night. It's a Friday, so Sandy and I won't have to worry about school the next day. It's the next step. Mr. Marquette said so."

"Mr. Marquette said so," Kelly mimicked maliciously.

"Mom—"

"Well, at least you're not calling that awful man 'Dad'—yet," Kelly murmured. She stood up before he could protest. "Go do your homework. You're still under eighteen, so I've still got my legal claws in you, and you've still got school tomorrow. Just because you've decided to run around making young innocents pregnant is no reason to stop going after those scholarships. In fact, it's all the more reason to work hard. So move. Now."

"Mom!"

"What?"

He had started up the stairs, but now he turned toward her, and for a minute he looked so mischievous that she was tempted to swat him.

"I don't run around making young innocents pregnant. Only one." He grinned.

"Go on, laugh!" she warned him seriously. "Jarod, you're in deep trouble, my love. You haven't even begun to realize just how deep."

His smile faded, and when he spoke, his voice was soft, yet reproachful and challenging. "Was I a 'disaster,' Mother?"

She bit her lip and didn't feel the pain, didn't realize until later when she tasted it that she had drawn blood. She felt the color drain from her cheeks, but she didn't look away from him, and it was her turn to answer coolly.

"Maybe I've been too honest with you, Jarod." She turned and left the room.

"Mom wait!"

He tried to call her back; he even started down the stairs. But Kelly had already retreated, stiff-backed, into her office, where she slammed the door, then locked it.

She sat down in front of her pictures, and started to cry again. It didn't seem fair. It just didn't seem fair. You worked so hard, tried so hard, and you just couldn't keep your children from repeating your own mistakes.

She stopped crying as numbness settled over her. She picked up her pencil. Her pictures of Marquette as Daryl were staring her in the face. Despairingly she tossed them to the floor and started over again.

She had to get her work finished. She had to. It was even more imperative now that she turn in quality material on time, and without the least hitch.

She was going to help Jarod and Sandy. If they chose to marry and have the child, she was going to help them as much as she could. They'd still have a hard, hard road.

Finally she was able to let her fingers take over, let them command her mind. Daryl had been backed up against the wall by the followers of the Fairy Queen; he knew he had no escape. Humbly he knelt before her; mercifully she decided not to throw him into the bottomless pit for all eternity.

Dreams, Kelly decided, were the strangest things, for even as she dreamed, she knew that it wasn't real, that it was a dream.

It began with the most beautiful swirl of mist, silver mist, going in circles, rising. And when the mist had risen she saw the ice: hard, sleek ice, covering the pond in the deep freeze of winter. She heard the sound that only skates can make over ice, and she saw them, herself and David, as they had been that day....

He had been a lot like Jarod. The same age, the same vitality. The same smile. And she had watched him. Watched him skating. Sliding gracefully, moving with supreme ease. Moving like magic across the ice, his smile touching her, her lips returning that smile....

She could see the two of them, when the ice show was over, talking and laughing. They had gone into Charleston to buy hamburgers and fries, and they hadn't touched, either. She barely remembered what they had said to each other. She could remember the feeling. The absolute longing.

She could remember going to the cabin, and laughing as she held out her hand, and the doe, not shy in the least, had come forward to nuzzle the peanuts from her palm.

And then they'd gone inside, where David had built a fire. She would never forget staring into his eyes in front of that fire, never forget how...

Kelly tossed and turned, then woke up with a start and stared into the darkness. She tossed her blankets aside and jumped to the floor, then went running down the hallway to Jarod's room.

He wasn't sleeping, though it wouldn't have mattered to her if he had been. Kelly flicked on the light and stared at her startled son.

"It was the cabin!" she accused him. "You went to my cabin!"

He didn't answer, his cheeks turned red.

"How could you?" Kelly asked reproachfully. "It was my cabin!"

"Mom," Jarod hesitated, "it was Dad's cabin. It isn't a shrine or a temple or anything. He would want—he would want us to use it, to be happy there."

"Not as ecstatic as you were!" Kelly said dryly. Jarod lowered his head, and she could see that he was trying to hide a grin. She knew exactly what he was thinking: You and Dad were pretty ecstatic there, too, huh?

He didn't say it. Kelly let out an oath and spun around to return to her own room. Amazing. She'd managed to get her work done. She'd showered and gone to bed. Jarod had finished his homework and gone to bed, too. Everything had been going along so normally....

Dinner. The next step—according to Marquette! Kelly slammed a fist into her pillow. Oh, Jarod! she thought again. Couldn't you have picked a girl with a more human father?

Eventually she fell back to sleep.

* * *

Dan Marquette sat with his feet up on his desk, his chair tilted back, his eyes on the amber swirl of Scotch against the ice in his glass. He lifted the glass to himself in mock salute.

"Fine bit of parenting there, Marquette. Fine, fine bit of parenting!"

He swallowed a gulp of Scotch and frowned because he didn't even shudder, and he began to wonder how much of the stuff he had already drunk. Not that much, was it? And have a heart, it wasn't every day a man learned that his baby, his daughter, his girl, his pride and joy, his greatest pleasure, was pregnant.

Pregnant. Really, honestly, pregnant.

"And to the fine, mature way you handled the situation!" Dan mocked himself, lifting his glass again. Listening to Sandy sob out her story, then running off half-cocked that way.

He grinned suddenly. Well, at least the boy's mother had been every bit as stunned as he had been. The boy's mother. She didn't look like more than a girl herself. She didn't look old enough to have a son who was almost eighteen. She didn't look anywhere large enough to have created such a child.

"Oh, Sandy!" Dan said softly.

He smiled ruefully; he didn't really have it in him anymore to blame either of them. He'd been ready to blame the boy—any father of a daughter was probably apt to do such a thing. But then he'd met Jarod McGraw, and he'd instantly liked him. Liked the way he'd stood up for Sandy, liked his honesty, his determination, his purpose. It might have been an absolutely horrible disaster, but maybe...

There was a soft rapping on his door. Sandy didn't wait for him to call her, but slipped in, running around to land on her knees by his chair and take his hand anxiously.

"Daddy?"

He smiled into her beseeching eyes. "I'm okay, sweetheart. How are you doing?"

She nodded and remained silent for a minute; then she lowered her head and asked, "Daddy, you like Jarod, don't you?"

"Yes, I do."

"Then everything is all right?"

"No, everything is still a mess. You two are too young for this. He's responsible and mature for his age, but that isn't going to help much. Not when you're both still in school. Not when a baby needs constant love and attention. Not when you're going to need a home at the same time as you're trying to buy textbooks that might cost as much as fifty dollars apiece."

"Daddy—"

She was going to start crying again. Dan was ready to kick himself. He placed his hands on her head and kissed her quickly, drawing her against him.

"Shush, shush, sweetheart! Everything is going to be okay. I love you, Sandy. No matter what, I love you! You know that. No matter what, I'll always be here."

She was smiling then, through her tears, a little pleased—a little relieved.

"You do like him, Dad?"

"Yes, I do like him."

"He's the best!"

"Sandy, he might be the best, but he's still only seventeen." Dan swung his feet to the ground suddenly and stood, then began to pace his office. Through the picture window in back he could see the mountains and the endless forests, and he found himself wondering: Where? Where did those two go? Was it the coming of spring that brought the death of innocence? Or was it something beautiful, something natural, something that I can't see because I'm her father? She seems to love him so much; they're both so sure. Isn't this what I should want for her? A love this deep?

Yes . . . it was just way too early.

She was watching him anxiously. He sighed. "Sandy, I'm still just . . . amazed, I guess." He went back to his chair and fell into it, staring at her. "I always thought that we were close. I thought I'd done a decent job with the birds and the bees. And for heaven's sake, Sandy, they've been teaching sex education in school for years now!"

Sandy flushed a brilliant pink, but she didn't turn away from him. "I got caught by the odds, Dad."

"The odds?"

"Yes. We were very careful. Only one in ten thousand would have gotten pregnant the way that I did. It was—"

"Wait, wait, wait!" Dan put up a hand, wincing. "Never mind! I thought I was raising a vestal virgin here! My fault, but I'm not up to the particulars here, okay?"

Sandy nodded. He gave her a kiss on the forehead. "Go to bed, huh?" he said huskily. "We'll discuss this tomorrow. You'll need your rest."

"I will?"

Dan rolled his eyes. "You haven't met your dear beloved's mother yet, have you?"

Sandy shook her head ruefully. "Does she hate me?"

Yes, I think she does! Dan thought, but he wasn't about to say that to Sandy. "She just has a few definite opinions, so you'd better be ready to listen—and defend yourself on cue!"

"That bad?" Sandy whispered.

Dan laughed, then grew sober. "No, she isn't that bad. She's...cute. I think I got us both off on the wrong foot by assuming that she was Jarod's sister. She was very indignant when I insisted on seeing her father."

"Oh, Dad! You didn't!"

"I did. Sandy, she can't be more than five-two, and I doubt she weighs a hundred pounds."

"Really?" Fascinated, Sandy curled up by his feet again. She frowned. "What else is she like?" Sandy laughed. "At least I'm bigger than she is! She won't be a physical threat!"

"I'm the only physical threat you need to worry about, young lady," her father chastised her. But he smiled suddenly. "We'll handle Mrs. McGraw, don't worry. She has enormous blue eyes—"

"Like Jarod's!"

"Hmm. Like Jarod's. And her hair is gold, like the sun. Like a wheat field, shimmering—"

Dan caught himself, realizing that his description was taking on a poetic edge. He glanced at Sandy quickly, but she was frowning, worrying only about what would take place between her and Kelly the next night.

"Sandy, go on to bed now, huh?" Dan repeated, keeping his voice at its strictest, most parental best.

"She's going to have a lot of things to say, good things for you both to listen to. You two are busy being in love, and neither one of you has spent two seconds thinking practically."

"Dad, you flew right off the handle—"

"Yes, I did. But I calmed down, and now we're all going to have to look at this thing from every angle. Now good night!"

Sandy stood up and started out of the room, smiled weakly, and closed the door behind her. Dan stayed in his office for a few minutes longer, then sighed, rose and followed her out. In the hallway, he paused. He could hear her crying, up in her room.

He climbed the stairs quickly to reach her.

She threw her arms around his neck. "Daddy, I'm so scared! I don't want Jarod to hate me. I don't want him to turn away from me! I'm afraid! I want to marry him right away, tomorrow, before he can discover that I'm not special."

"Shush. You *are* special, princess!"

Dan rocked her back and forth, assuring her that Jarod McGraw was very much in love with her, and that things would work out, but only if they were aware of all their options. He kept talking to her, softly, until she sniffed and shuddered, and at last fell asleep.

Only then did Dan leave her.

He went back downstairs, down to the huge modern kitchen that overlooked the mountains. He thought about young Jarod McGraw, and he thought about Jarod's mother.

"Damn!" Dan muttered, suddenly feeling fiercely protective. "You think it was all Sandy's fault, huh? You're the one raising the young stud there, ma'am!"

Then Dan laughed out loud. They were young; they were in love. No one was at fault.

But Mrs. McGraw was going to have to see it that way, too, he decided. He smiled slightly, envisioning the night that was to come. The battle that he was about to join.

She really was just a little bit of a thing. But her fighting spirit was keen. He thought about the way her eyes had flashed, the way her blond ponytail had looked like liquid sunlight.

She was a pretty woman. No, not just pretty. She had elegance, for all her casual appearance. She was delicate but strong. Those eyes of hers, so brilliantly blue, and fringed by such dark lashes, though she was so blond. Unique. There was something arresting about her face. Something alluring, something in her smile...

A smile that was warm and giving and honest—like Jarod's, Dan found himself admitting wryly. He really did like the boy, and he felt he understood why Sandy had fallen under his spell. He had those eyes... and that smile.

Dan decided to have another Scotch. At first he told himself that he didn't need it, but then he decided that he definitely did. Tomorrow was going to be a rough day.

He would protect Sandy; she would protect Jarod. And then there was Mrs. McGraw...

Dan grinned suddenly, lacing his fingers behind his head and stretching out in a smug fashion.

"Why, Mrs. McGraw!" he murmured. "I think I've got your number! And if I have to, I *will* use it."

Chapter 3

"**Y**ou're not going to wear *that*, are you?"

Halfway down the stairs, Kelly paused and turned slowly, suspiciously, to face her son, her eyes narrowing.

"What's the matter with what I'm wearing, Jarod?"

"You look like—you look like someone's mother," he said unhappily.

"Jarod, I *am* someone's mother."

"Grandmother, then. Mom, you look like a nun."

Kelly smiled vaguely and continued down the stairway. She didn't look that prim, and she knew it. Her skirt was long and her blouse had a Chinese collar, but it was soft and silky in a teal blue that was becoming to her eyes and hair.

"Jarod, my outfit is fine," she called lightly to him over her shoulder. "You're determined to marry Sandra, and I don't want to meet my prospective daughter-in-law looking like Bubbles La Tour."

"Well, you don't have to look like Sister Margaret-Mary, either!" Jarod protested.

"Get the car, dear," Kelly said serenely.

He gave her one last exasperated glance, then gave up and went out to get the car. Kelly turned to the hallway mirror to give herself a quick once-over.

Was she dressed—too old? Maybe, but her height was such a drawback when she was trying to stand her ground, and she had to stand her ground—maturely—tonight.

She had her hair piled on top of her head, but it was soft, fine hair, and little wisps of it were spilling about her face already. Her heels were three inches high, but she still felt short. "That's your fault, Jarod!" she said heatedly. It was impossible to feel tall when he towered over her.

He beeped the horn, and she gave herself a little shake. Face it, she told herself wryly, she wasn't out to impress the young lovers with her age and wisdom. Marquette had mistaken her for a child at their first meeting, and she was vehemently determined to prove to that obnoxious individual that she was not—in the least—a child.

She smiled grimly, knowing full well that he wondered how old she really was. "I should tell him that I'm sixty," she said. "And that Jarod was an accident late in life!"

The horn beeped again, and she shrugged and hurried out the door. Jarod watched her as she climbed in beside him, but she pretended not to notice. He was so anxious. Well, she wasn't going to let him off the hook so easily. He was just going to have to be anxious for a while. After all, she was a nervous wreck.

Why was she so upset? she wondered. True, she had some definite opinions, and yes, a few things to say that she hoped were infinitely wise and just might help. But as to the situation, well . . .

There were worse things that could have happened. Jarod was alive and well. He hadn't been in a terrible accident; he hadn't gotten drunk and driven off a mountain. He wasn't a dope addict.

He had just gotten a girl pregnant, and at least he still seemed to be in love with her. And she would probably turn out to be a decent young lady.

No, Kelly could handle the situation.

Marquette was the fly in the ointment. He simply rubbed her entirely the wrong way.

Kelly clenched her teeth and looked down at her hands. What difference did that make? It was Jarod's life she had to worry about tonight. She had to meet Sandy, had to get to know Sandy, not her overbearing father.

Kelly roused herself enough to watch where they were going. They twisted and curved up the mountain until they came to a driveway overhung with foliage and seeming to lead nowhere.

It didn't, of course. Kelly gasped at her first sight of the house. It seemed to rise naturally from the mountain, all granite and redwood and glass, immense and beautiful. From the driveway she could see the living room, with its walls of glass, and through that glass the stone fireplace, the warm earth tones of the Indian rugs and casual furniture.

"It's nice, isn't it?" Jarod demanded a little smugly.

Kelly turned on him. "I thought Marquette was some kind of historian. You didn't tell me that he was well-off. And don't you dare sound so smug. This doesn't change anything."

"Mom, you're just so worried about money! We won't starve. Don't you see—"

"If you take a penny of his money, Jarod, I will be so disappointed in you that I'll—I'll scream."

He laughed softly and reminded her, "You were going to give me money for college. A lot of parents do."

"That's different."

"Mother—"

"Drop it, Jarod, and let's go in before I change my mind!"

He decided that she was serious. With a sigh he walked around the car to escort her out. Kelly already felt tense and miserable.

The front door opened before they could reach it. Marquette was standing there. Kelly hesitated on the path; only Jarod's touch got her moving again.

Marquette looked . . . good.

Really good. He had on a light, casual jacket, a shirt open at the neck, and nicely tailored trousers. His hair had just been washed. She could tell, because it was still damp against his forehead. He smiled when she came nearer, a deep, inviting smile. She realized with a bit of a shock that he was handsome, very hand-some, and that his smile was more than inviting—it was dangerous. With those dark eyes of his and the white slash of his smile against his bronzed, rugged features, he was alluring . . . and exciting!

"Jarod, Mrs. McGraw, come in. Mrs. McGraw, I assume that you're quite anxious to meet Sandy."

Yes, of course, she was anxious to meet Sandy. But shock had done cruel things to her, Kelly decided. Marquette took her hand in one of his big ones, and his scent, not so much after-shave as some kind of clean, woodsy soap, seemed to wash over her. She wanted to shriek, let go of my hand! And of course it was worse, because even in heels she still had to tilt her head back to meet his sardonic smile.

"Mom," Jarod prodded her. "This is Sandy."

Kelly didn't know what she had been expecting. Maybe some sultry Mata Hari who had led her upstanding innocent son astray. A natural reaction, perhaps. But Sandy was, quite simply, beautiful, and far more innocent-looking than Kelly could ever have expected. She was dark, like her father, with beautiful, big dark eyes, and dark hair with a touch of red that made it one of the richest shades of auburn that Kelly had ever seen. She wore it long, with no concession to fad or fashion. She was tall, too. About five-foot-nine—a beautiful height against Jarod's size, but—irritating!

The whole damn world suddenly seemed to be tall! Kelly felt a bit like Alice in Wonderland. Here she was, so tiny, with a bunch of normal-sized people, as if she had eaten something strange.

"Sandy, how do you do?"

She offered the words softly, and gave the girl her hand with a nice smile. How could you be so perfect? she thought in despair. You've ruined his life! He could have had his choice of colleges. . . .

"Come in," Marquette said. "We're all here. Can I get you a drink?"

"No!" she said sharply. What did he think this was, a social occasion? Of course, she told herself, it *was* a social occasion; they were all trying to get to know each other, and she actually did want a drink.

"Ah, yes, thank you," she murmured easily a moment later.

Unlike her, Dan Marquette seemed to be perfectly at ease, even amused. "Come into the kitchen with me, Mrs. McGraw."

He didn't wait for her reply, just started across the vast living room with the wonderful glass walls and inviting fireplace.

Sandy and Jarod were staring at each other, oblivious to the fact that anyone else was around. Kelly glanced at them uneasily, then followed Dan Marquette.

The kitchen, too, was beautifully contemporary. Cool light oak European cabinetry, a big butcherblock island, restaurant range, rows of gleaming copper pots, and a booth against another glass wall.

Kelly wandered over to the window. Something smelled wonderful, though she didn't know what was cooking. Dan pulled glasses from the cabinets, then got ice from the freezer. Kelly could feel him watching her all the while.

"What will you have?"

She shook her head. "It doesn't matter. Wine. A wine spritzer or a cooler, something like that."

He poured wine and soda over ice and offered her the glass, searching her eyes, his own amusement so evident that Kelly snapped at him. "I can't begin to see what you find so funny."

"You, Mrs. McGraw."

"Oh, really?"

"Yes. You are appalled that we've left the children together. Alone."

"Yes, I guess I am," Kelly replied coolly.

"Aren't you trying to close the barn door with the horse long gone?"

"Are you trying to encourage outrageous behavior?"

"Not so outrageous. Natural, I believe."

"Natural! You're making them sound like salmon who will just automatically swim upstream—"

"Just how old are you, Mrs. McGraw?"

"What?" Kelly gasped in horror. She hadn't been prepared for that attack—not at all. Of course, it had been bound to come.

"How old are you, Mrs. McGraw? It's a legitimate question, under the circumstances."

"It's none of your business!"

"Oh, but I think it is. You're sitting there condemning the hell out of those kids, when you were apparently running around yourself at a very young age—"

"It's none of your business!" Kelly repeated in fury. She slammed her glass down on the counter with such vehemence that it shattered, but she barely noticed. She stared at Marquette, then turned to leave.

He caught her arm, whirling her back around. "Stop it, Mrs. McGraw. You—"

"Let go of me! I knew this was a mistake. I'm leaving."

"No, you're not."

"I'm not staying—"

"Oh, but you are! Aren't you here for your son's welfare?"

"I am—"

Kelly broke off and lifted her chin to stare at him. The insolence of this man! She looked from his face to his hand, hard upon her shoulder. She drew in a deep breath with all the dignity she could muster.

"Excuse me, Mr. Marquette. Would you mind...?"

He wasn't offended. Nor did he release her. He simply grinned. "Dan."

"What?"

"Mr. Marquette sounds awfully formal, under the circumstances. My name is Dan. And yours...?"

"Mine is Mrs. McGraw, Mr. Marquette."

He started to laugh. To her horror he touched her cheek, drawing a fine, quivering line along her face to her chin.

"You're just a kid yourself, aren't you?" he asked softly. "That makes this whole thing very hard."

She stared at him, mesmerized, for a very long second. At last she realized her position, so close to him that their bodies were almost touching, his hand on her shoulder, his other still lingering on her face. It was...intimate. And it was, she knew deep down inside herself somewhere...nice.

Nice!

That touch, so strong, so devastatingly male. His voice, hard and masculine. His scent, so clean, so male, as rugged as his mountain...

She wrenched away from him. "Mr. Marquette, I'm not a kid. I'm unhappy about this entire situation because it's going to be very, very hard on those two children!"

He listened to her, then cocked his head and turned quickly away, and Kelly knew that he was amused again. He moved into the pantry and came back with a broom, and she saw that he meant to clean up the glass that she had shattered. She didn't move to help him, but she didn't move to leave again, either.

"No. Marquette, you don't seem to understand."

"I understand," he said bluntly, stooping down to sweep up the broken glass. "I understand perfectly. They were attracted to each other. It happens at that age. They carried that attraction to its instinctive conclusion, and they just happened to get caught. Lady, if you don't think I went crazy at first, you've missed the boat. But then, I'm starting to get that impression about you anyway. How the hell do you think I felt?"

"You're a man—"

"Yeah, that's exactly how I felt. Like a man— whose sweet, innocent daughter had been taken. That's why I burst into your house the way I did. Instinct, Mrs. McGraw. I wanted to kill. Well, I was wrong. Your son is a nice kid. He and Sandy are really in love with each other. There was nothing sordid about what they did. They fell in love. And they're still in love. I was afraid he was going to be some kind of love 'em and leave 'em jock, but—"

"Oh, you know the type well, huh?" Kelly jeered, interrupting. This wasn't going well at all. She had wanted to be so mature, but she wasn't handling things—he was!

"Nice strike, lady, nice strike. Why? Were you caught by that particular type? Did your father have to aim a shotgun at Mr. McGraw to get the two of you down the aisle?"

He paused in his clean-up effort and stared straight at her as he asked the question. Kelly was sorry she had broken her glass. She would have loved to dump the wine right over his head.

In fact, the urge was so strong that she decided to go for his glass. She reached for it in sudden frenzy.

But he was prepared. His arm shot out, and his fingers caught her wrist in a twisting, vise-like grip.

"What a temper. A few more years might cure it!" he warned her.

"Too bad nothing will ever cure you!" she retorted, pulling away from his grasp. As she did so, she slipped on the wet floor and fell to her knees. She winced sharply; she'd knelt on glass, and it had cut into her knee.

Marquette was instantly concerned, and he put his hand on her shoulder again.

"Just let me go. The glass—"

But he didn't let her go. He stood, and she found herself swept up into his strong arms. Instinctively she wound her own arms around his neck for balance. He held her easily with one arm and touched the wound with his free hand. "Oh, damn. I'm sorry."

"It's nothing."

"It's deep."

He set her down at the table and quickly reached into a cabinet for antiseptic and a bandage. He knelt down beside her again, touching her wound carefully.

"It's nothing, really."

"The stocking has to go," he murmured, his hand on her leg. Kelly, crimson and mortified and certain that he meant to remove her stocking himself, leaped up, quickly finding her garter and releasing the offending garment. Marquette removed her shoe and began to slide the stocking down her leg.

It was just then that Jarod and Sandy made their appearance in the kitchen.

"Mother!" Jarod said.

"Dad...?" Sandy queried.

Kelly felt color flooding her entire body. She was sitting, Dan Marquette at her feet. Her stocking was in his hand, her bare leg resting over his knee. She wanted to die....

Dan didn't seem to be upset in the least.

"Your mom's glass broke," he said smoothly, dropping the stocking and picking up the antiseptic. "She cut her knee."

Kelly was sure that she could have heard a pin drop, but Dan Marquette was still undaunted. He daubed the antiseptic on her knee with straightforward attention, murmuring that it would be all right when she inhaled sharply at the stinging pain.

"Is it okay, Mom?" Jarod asked anxiously, moving over to her.

"Oh, yes, really, it's not that bad. I, uh, I—"

"Sandy, do me a favor, please, will you?" Marquette asked his daughter. "Finish picking up that glass before someone else gets cut. Jarod, why don't you make your mom another spritzer?"

Sandy obediently began to clean up the broken glass and spilled wine, while Jarod made Kelly a drink and brought it over to her. She sipped it quickly, and her vision swam for a moment. All she saw was that dark masculine head bent over her knee, and she was nearly overwhelmed by the impulse to run her fingers through that thick hair. They actually itched...her fingers itched. It would be so natural to touch him.

"There, that should do it." Marquette looked up at her. He was smiling. A devilish smile, a fascinating smile. She returned his stare. Don't! Don't you do this to me, she insisted silently. You won't get away with it, I'm not a kid, and I'm not about to fall for you, no matter how masculine and charming you think you are!

He merely shrugged, and his grin deepened. Then he rose.

"Jarod, the salad is in the refrigerator. Sandy, you check on the roast and the potatoes."

Sandy laughed. "Hey, Dad! What's your job here, huh?"

He laughed in return. "I'm going to help Mrs. McGraw hobble out to the table. That other shoe really needs to go, too."

Kelly didn't get a chance to protest. He was already slipping off her second shoe.

"How do you ever walk in these things, anyway? he demanded.

"I manage fine," Kelly retorted.

He grinned, offering her his hand.

"Her name is Kelly," Jarod offered.

"Kelly," Dan Marquette murmured, staring at her warmly. "Nice. Fitting. Irish ... green."

"Short," Jarod teased.

"Jarod!" Kelly gave him a sharp warning. But Jarod didn't notice it, or maybe he did, but felt that he was safe.

Kelly swallowed back another retort. She wanted to help these kids as badly as Marquette did, but really! They should have been responsible, and they should feel somewhat chastised this evening. Instead, they were having a good time—at her expense.

Marquette's hand was out, though, and she had little choice but to accept it. He led her out—barefoot—to the dining room, a beautiful room, all in glass, like the living room, and simply decorated in an Oriental style. Kelly looked around while Jarod set out the salad—a really nice salad for a single man, she had to admit. Unless, of course, Sandy had made it. Sandy brought out hot rolls, while Jarod disappeared, then reappeared with sodas for the two of them. Finally everyone was seated.

Jarod glanced at Dan Marquette and his mother, then mouthed out a quick grace. Then, being Jarod— a healthy and still-growing young man—he commented on how delicious the food was. Kelly found herself echoing the sentiment, then asking Dan whether he or Sandy had done the cooking.

"Neither," he responded. "Reeves is the cook."

"Reeves had been with us all my life," Sandy explained to Kelly. "What is he, Dad? Sort of a gentleman's gentleman, I suppose. After all these years he's still very proper and very British. He's great. He's the best 'mum' any girl ever had." Sandy waved a hand in the air. "Dad and I are chaotic at best, but everything runs smoothly because of Reeves."

Kelly watched Sandy, smiling. It was so ridiculous! Here they were carrying on this polite and normal conversation, and the long-haired, innocent little beauty sitting across from her was pregnant with her grandchild!

Kelly heard herself ask Sandy where Reeves was, and Sandy explained that he had his own room at the back of the house.

"He needs a certain independence," she explained.

"I think we're all done with our salad," Dan murmured. Sandy and Jarod jumped to their feet together and collected the plates.

As if everything had been choreographed, Kelly thought. And it had been. It felt like "them" against "her."

The kids disappeared into the kitchen. Kelly felt Dan Marquette staring at her, and she looked over at him inquiringly.

"What's wrong?" he asked her.

"Wrong?" She sipped her spritzer, then sat back in her chair and laughed. "Wrong?" She had to be careful; her voice was threatening to rise hysterically. "What could be wrong? Those two are children, with no apparent sense of right or wrong or responsibility, and they're going to have a child. Unless—"

"Unless?" Marquette said sharply. He was smiling, but his dark eyes were narrowed as he leaned closer to her. "Unless? What are you suggesting, Mrs. McGraw? That Sandra have an abortion?"

His blunt suggestion made her color again, and Kelly had to inhale slowly in order to reply. She was too furious at his assumption to even bother setting him straight.

"I'm thinking of your daughter more than I'm thinking of my son," she said flatly. "Both their lives will have to change, but trust me, it's the woman who has the child. Sandy will bear the brunt of whatever comes."

He leaned back again, watching her, idly running his fingers down his glass. Kelly found herself watching those fingers and trembling inside.

"I think you're missing the main point here, Kelly. These two know what they're going to do. We can be their friends or their enemies, but we can't change their minds."

Sandy came back into the dining room with a smile on her face that quickly faded when she saw the way that the adults were looking at each other.

Jarod sailed back in carrying a huge platter of parsleyed potatoes and broccoli in cheese sauce. His smile faded, too.

Kelly looked down at her plate when Dan stood up to carve the roast. She found herself becoming vaguely aware that he had started using her first name when he asked for her plate and piled it high with food.

They all sat down to eat in silence. Kelly felt that since she had caused the discomfort, she ought to alleviate it. But all she could think of saying was, "Everything is really delicious."

"Thank you," Marquette said stiffly.

"Mrs. McGraw, your glass is empty," Sandy said softly. "Can I fix you another drink?"

Kelly sat back, smiling at the girl who would soon be her daughter-in-law. "Are you trying to ply me with liquor? Ask Jarod—my tongue just gets sharper."

Sandy flushed and laughed, and Jarod assured her that they were going to hear from his mother one way or another that evening, anyway. Dan Marquette stood up, excused himself and disappeared with both glasses. He returned with them refilled, and Kelly suddenly felt more comfortable, though she couldn't have said why. She stared at Sandy bluntly.

"Sandy, I'll start off with the tough stuff. I admit that I'm deeply disappointed in both of you. You seem like a lovely young lady, but what you did was—"

"Mother," Jarod interrupted uncomfortably. "Come on! We're seniors. Everyone—"

"Everyone?" Kelly murmured, watching them both. "'Everyone' isn't expecting a child, and 'everyone'—"

"All right," Jarod interjected. "What do you want, Mom? A blow-by-blow description of how we let it happen?"

"Jarod!"

"Well, Mom, we weren't planning what happened the first time!"

"You were careless and irresponsible!" Kelly retorted, her son's attitude pushing her temper higher. "And now you act like you're being Mr. Magnanimous, Jarod! Sandy is going to do the majority of the paying—have you really thought about that? Sandy, have *you* thought about it? I can't change your minds, can't make you do anything, and I'll be honest, I don't know what the 'right' thing really is. But, Sandy, you have options. You don't have to have this baby—and neither your father, Jarod nor I has the right to make you!"

Sandy had gone ashen. Marquette looked as if he were about to explode and Jarod seemed ready to strangle his mother, but Kelly kept going. This was for Sandy, between the two of them as women, and she didn't feel that either Jarod or Dan had the right to interrupt her until she was done.

"Or you could have the baby and give it up for adoption."

"Oh, my God!" Sandy whispered, close to tears.

Marquette's chair slid back along the floor, but Kelly ignored the sound and leaned closer to the girl.

"I wouldn't want that, Sandy. That baby is my grandchild. To be honest, what I want is for you and Jarod to marry each other. It's just that it's going to be hard, Sandy. Miserably hard. I want you and Jarod to see that; I want you both to see your options, and then, Sandy, once you two make your decision, I swear that I'll back you and help you in any way that I can. If I've hurt you, I'm sorry."

There was silence, complete silence. Then Sandy burst into tears and stood up to race from the room. Jarod hopped to his feet, cast Kelly a cold stare and raced after her.

From somewhere Kelly heard a clock chime. Dan Marquette was still, dead still, but Kelly couldn't look at him.

She heard him rise, heard him walk over to the window. Felt him when he turned to watch her in silence once again.

"What? What!" Kelly shrieked at last. "Are you going to rip into me for hurting your daughter? Get it over with. Go ahead. Everything that I said was important and—"

"Yes, it was."

"What?"

Startled, Kelly stared at him. He was smiling at her. "It *is* going to be hard, and it *is* important that they think about what they're doing."

"Oh..."

He came back to the table and sat down next to her. Kelly instantly felt as if the temperature in the room had risen by ten degrees. He wasn't touching her, he wasn't even very close, but she could feel him. Could feel his smile, feel those dark eyes.

"You don't want to talk to me, Kelly McGraw, but I'd have to be blind not to know that you were ridiculously young when you had Jarod. How old are you now? Thirty-five?"

"Forty-five!" Kelly lied quickly.

He only laughed again. "Thirty-six? Thirty-four? Things went badly for you—I'm sorry. But you should know that things that start off well can go badly, too. Sandy was planned, Kelly. Her mother and I met in college; we got married right after graduation. Sandy was born a year after our wedding day. Perfect planning. Or so I thought. Well, her mother left when Sandy was five days old. So much for planning. I think that Jarod loves Sandy—and I know that she loves him. Yes, it's going to be hard. Let's help them make it, shall we?''

She turned slowly to stare at him. At the dark eyes gazing so intently into her own. At that smile. That charming, masculine, diabolical smile.

His hand was stretched toward her. He wanted her to take it.

Kelly stared from his hand to his eyes, and then back to his hand again.

''We still haven't gotten anywhere here,'' she murmured. ''They have to finish their senior year. Sandy is going to get more and more pregnant—''

''Pregnant is pregnant,'' Marquette interrupted dryly. ''She can't get any more pregnant than she already is. She can just get closer to giving birth.''

''That's what I mean! We have to decide how to—how to handle this!''

Kelly looked at him, suddenly wide-eyed with confusion. There really was so much to do! A wedding, a place to live, college, and on and on . . .

''It will go much better'' Marquette murmured, ''if you and I are friends. Don't you think?''

His hand closed over hers, and Kelly stared at it. She felt his power, his warmth.

No, she thought. No, no, no . . .

She realized that she was afraid to be his friend. He would demand a great deal of a . . . friend.

Chapter 4

Kelly let herself into the house smiling. She didn't know why she felt so much better about things—she just did.

"Jarod!"

He came running down the stairs when he heard her, a pencil stuck behind his ear. That made her feel better, too. He hadn't forgotten about his schoolwork.

She could even admit that since everything had come out in the open, especially since they'd gone to the Marquettes' for dinner, Jarod had been doing better than ever in everything. Straight A's in school, and a note from the coach stating that by the time the season was over, Jarod would be able to attend the college of his choice on an athletic scholarship alone.

"Well?" he asked her anxiously.

She smiled, glad of the absurdly light feeling that had gripped her. Well, why not? Sandy Marquette was pregnant, and she was very definitely going to be

Sandra McGraw soon enough. It would be foolish, Kelly decided, not to enjoy her only son's wedding. Especially when Sandy needed her so much! Sandy had called her three times for advice already. Reeves—the "gentleman's gentleman"—might have been able to keep the house running smoothly, but he didn't seem to be quite the perfect substitute mother for a young bride.

"Mom?" Jarod prompted impatiently.

Kelly smiled, throwing her arms open to him. "The priest says that the first Saturday in June will be fine. I think it's perfect, don't you?"

"Super!"

He accepted her embrace, then swept her off her feet to whirl her around the hallway.

"Jarod!" Kelly shrieked breathlessly, but even as she gasped he was setting her down, staring at her worriedly.

"Well, what did he say? Did you tell him that Sandy... I mean, did you explain that we, ah—"

"I didn't lie, Jarod," Kelly told him quietly. But she couldn't help grinning. "The man is a Roman Catholic priest, Jarod, so he was glad that you and Sandra are going to get married."

"By June..."

"By June Sandy will be about four and a half months along, from what she's told me. Not necessarily noticeable at all." Kelly shrugged. "If people know, they know. If they don't—well, we won't announce it. Oh, Jarod, come on! You're both so young. This is a once in a lifetime affair. Sandy should have a beautiful white dress and a mile-long train, the whole nine yards."

Jarod lowered his eyes, then looked up at her anxiously. "You think so? You really think so?"

"Definitely."

He hugged her again, so tightly that she had to fight his embrace. Jarod didn't always know his own strength.

"You'd better be careful doing that to Sandy!" Kelly remonstrated, but she was glad of his happiness. A little pang tore at her heart, and she realized that half of what hurt her so badly was that she just wasn't ready to see him grow up. Still, he was her only child. And she was going to do her damnedest to see that his wedding was perfect. If the gossips wanted to talk, they were welcome to do so. She wouldn't change a thing. She would see that Sandy's gown was the whitest white imaginable.

Because to her, Sandy remained pure. The more she talked to the girl, the more convinced she became that Sandy loved Jarod with all her heart. And there was nothing in the world more pure, more innocent—more holy!—than a love like that.

"Sandy will be thrilled," Jarod said.

"Why don't you call her and tell her?"

"She's on her way over now."

"Now? Why?"

"Oh—I forgot. They're both coming."

"Both? Who both?"

Kelly knew what he was talking about, of course. She just wasn't so sure that she wanted to know.

"Sandy and Dan."

"Dan?" Kelly said disapprovingly.

Jarod grinned. "It's too early to call him 'Dad,' isn't it? And Mr. Marquette sounds absurd. And Sandy calls you Kelly."

Kelly had no reply to that. "Why are they coming over?"

"Because we're all going out," Jarod said happily.

Kelly shook her head. "Uh-uh! We're not all going out. You all can go out, but—"

"Mom, I said that you would go. I told him that you loved tubing, that you loved anything to do with the water."

"Jarod, you can't run around telling—"

"Mom, please, for my sake, for Sandy's sake. Come on, they've just moved here. From D.C. Going tubing is new and exciting for them."

"That's just wonderful. I'm excited for them. And you are more than welcome to go have an exciting time with them. Just don't run around agreeing to things—"

"Mom, please, just this once."

"No!"

Jarod hung his shoulders slightly; he seemed to give up. Kelly felt a moment's satisfaction, but then Jarod started in again.

"You love tubing. And if it were just Sandy and me, you'd come along in a minute. You're afraid of him, that's what it is."

"How dare you!"

"You're afraid of him!" he said loudly and clearly, staring at her.

"I am *not* afraid of him!"

"Then why won't you come?"

"Because. Because—"

The doorbell chose that precise minute to ring. Kelly stared at Jarod; Jarod stared at her.

"Because I'm busy!" Kelly snapped. Then since she was closest to the door, she went to answer it, throwing it open with a vengeance.

Sandy, her beautiful dark eyes bright with pleasure, greeted her. She was in a bathing suit, and she looked so young and lovely that Kelly had to smile, all too aware of how her son could have fallen so head over heels in love.

"Oh! You're not ready!" Sandy said, disappointed.

Kelly smiled. "I'm not coming, Sandy. I've really got an awful lot to do."

"Oh, come on! Please. You have to come. Dad just got the tubes. And he already dropped off the meat for the barbecue at the cottage. Please? He won't come if you don't."

"Well, I'm sorry—" Kelly began.

"What's wrong?"

She was interrupted by the man himself, or the devil himself, as she was beginning to think of him. He was in a pair of cutoffs that left very little to the imagination.

How the hell old are *you*? she wondered a little belligerently, unaware that she was staring at him. At his bare chest. Thickly covered with hair and hard with muscle.

He should have been skinny! Skinny and sickly looking! Weren't scholars supposed to be pale and scrawny and wear horn-rims and...

"Is something the matter?" he asked.

"No, I'm just a little busy today, that's all."

He shrugged, not pressing the point. To her surprise, Kelly was disappointed. *I don't want him to beg!*

she thought. But she had. She liked seeing him at any disadvantage, because . . .

Jarod was right, in a way. She wasn't afraid of Dan Marquette, but he did make her nervous.

"What a shame. The kids had said that you could go. I guess I'll stay home, too. Third wheel, you know."

"That's foolish," Kelly protested. "Sandy said you'd gotten all kinds of things for a barbecue at some cottage."

"I bought a little house along the Shenandoah. It's a shack, nothing more. I'm just fascinated by the river and the white water and everything."

Kelly kept smiling. "All the more reason why you should go."

Jarod came up behind Kelly and bent his head to whisper in her ear. "See, Mom, if you don't go, he won't go. And Sandy and I will be all alone. At a house. On the river. Half-naked."

She spun around. "Not amusing, Jarod. You're in no position to be giving me that kind of grief, young man."

He grinned, grabbed Sandy's arm and seemed to melt away.

"We'll be in the car, Dad!" Sandy called.

Kelly stared after them. "They should be locked in their rooms, the pair of them!"

"The problem, as I see it, was that they were perfectly content to be locked in a room—together." He lifted his shoulders in a shrug. "What are you going to do? They're too big to be spanked." He was silent for a moment. "They'll be paying enough. No movies, no dances, no fraternities or sororities. Let them enjoy each other now."

Kelly looked down at the floor. He was right. They were still children, delighting in little things. Harsh reality was already on its way, and if they could stay married in the face of it, they would have created a miracle.

"Are you coming or not?" Marquette asked her very softly. He was still smiling slightly. Ironically, ruefully—challengingly. She returned his gaze, wondering at his thoughts.

Damn him! He knew darn well that he made her uneasy. That she was much more aware of him as a man than she wanted to be. That his bluntness and his honesty and his very male physique were unnerving to her.

He even seemed to know that in many ways she was far more of an innocent than Sandy.

"Can't handle the big time, huh?" he dared her softly.

She certainly couldn't let herself retreat after that. "Step inside, Mr. Marquette," she said smoothly. "I'll just be a moment."

He grinned and did so. Inadvertently, Kelly stepped back, and his grin deepened.

"I don't bite, Mrs. McGraw."

"I never thought you did."

"Never?"

"Never."

"Really? I don't frighten you?"

"Not in the least."

"I'm so glad to hear that. Should I be encouraged? Do you actually like me?"

Kelly smiled sweetly. "I don't dislike you, Mr. Marquette. But then, I don't particularly. . . like you, either. Quite honestly, I don't really think about you one way or the other. If you'll excuse me, I'll run up and change."

"Please do."

"Make yourself at home."

"Thanks. I will."

Kelly turned regally, leaving him alone in the hallway. She resented the fact that he undoubtedly *would* make himself completely at home.

"Damn you, Dan Marquette!" she said, seething. "Bursting in here, taking charge. You'll get yours. I promise."

She dug through her bottom drawer and stared at her array of three bathing suits. One was a bikini, one a more modest athletic type, and the third, also a one-piece, was a shocking teal blue that drew out the color of her eyes. It had a low-cut front and very high-cut thighs.

"Do I or don't I?" she murmured. And then she grinned, thinking that two could play his game. She might be short, but all her pieces went together fairly well, and the bathing suit *was* extremely flattering. One of Jarod's friends had even tried to get a date with her when she had worn it for a school picnic down along the river.

"All right, Marquette, watch out!" She laughed to her reflection in the mirror as she dressed, and then she paused, startled to find that she was shockingly out of breath, that she felt all hot and trembly, and that she was as excited as a high school kid herself.

She closed her eyes and swallowed painfully, suddenly determined to ignore any challenge—to run. She had come too far, she was too old, she was too stable now, to take any risks. She had survived too much to start over....

"Hey! What are you doing up there?"

"Coming!"

Kelly gave herself a little shake and decided not to change out of her rather risqué bathing suit. She slipped an oversize T-shirt over it instead, then slid into an old pair of sneakers and went back downstairs.

She frowned because he wasn't in the hallway, but she sensed that he hadn't left the house. "Marquette?" she demanded sharply.

"In here."

The voice came from her office. Kelly strode uneasily to the doorway and stared in.

He was perched on top of her work stool, looking down at her drafting board. He had definitely made himself comfortable; he'd been in her refrigerator and was idly cradling a beer in his palm while he stared down at her work.

"What—" Kelly began, but then she broke off, because his eyes met hers and seemed to burn with a diabolical darkness. She couldn't tell if he was angry or amused, but he was certainly *something*.

And then she knew. Her idle drawings of Daryl the Devilish Dragon with his face were right on top.

"I should sue you for this," he murmured lightly. "Isn't this slander, or something like that?"

"It isn't anything!" Kelly said heatedly, rushing into the room. She snatched at the top picture, mortified to see that Esmeralda the Fairy Queen was flogging Daryl. And she hadn't done it on purpose, but Esmeralda did resemble her a bit and, well, Daryl was beyond a doubt the spitting image of Dan Marquette.

His hand landed on the picture when she tried to sweep it away, and his eyes caught hers again. "You don't think about me at all, huh? Not one way or the other?"

"*No!* What the hell are you doing in here?"

"You told me to make myself comfortable."

"I didn't tell you to snoop."

"I'm not snooping. I just ambled on in here to take a peek at your work."

"Well, you've peeked! Now get out!"

He grinned very slowly and smugly, releasing the paper and crossing his arms over his chest. He sipped the beer, watching her. "Kind of kinky, don't you think?" he finally asked.

"Not in the least. You should have been shot, the way you barged in here that first day."

"Shot. Clean, neat. An execution performed by a firing squad. But what we have here . . ."

His voice faded off insinuatingly, and when she crumpled the paper into a ball, he laughed.

"That's it! You're living in a fantasy world. 'Dark of the Moon.' Evildoers are punished with a flogging, the fairies rule, and daylight always comes. Nothing is real. No true problems—"

"Since you showed up, I've had nothing *but* problems!" Kelly snapped. "Would you get off my stool, please, and out of my office!"

"Certainly, certainly." He got up, but, maddeningly, he was still grinning. Worse still, he reached for her elbow to escort her out.

"Don't touch me!"

"What are you going to do? Flog me?"

"I'd like to—"

"What? I'm dying to hear it."

"I'd like to drown you! Shall we go, please?"

"'Please,' I love it! Yes, let's go. Before you chicken out and realize that I'm not a fantasy."

"What?"

Kelly stopped to stare up at him. He gripped her arm more tightly and gave it a little tug. "Come on, will you? The kids will be baked out there in the truck."

"Oh!"

Kelly groaned, but followed him. It was true—they'd been in the house for what seemed like forever, and the kids would surely be anxious, or worse, wondering what their parents were up to.

But when they reached Dan Marquette's truck neither Sandy nor Jarod seemed to have missed them in the least. Jarod—with all his size and length—was perched in the little well in back of the single seat to leave the other three room. Sandy was in the center, turned around on her knees, and together they were poring over a social sciences book. Dan left Kelly at the passenger door to walk around to the driver's side, and as she stood there, Kelly bit her lip, feeling another pang of regret assail her. They seemed so normal, Jarod and Sandy, so...young! Too young to drink legally, too young to vote, too young...

And Sandy looked much too chaste. So slim in her bathing suit. So innocent. They couldn't possibly be about to become parents.

"Are you getting in?"

Dan Marquette reached across his daughter to open the door. "Need a stepladder?" he teased.

"I can make it," Kelly shot back.

"Dad, you could have helped her!" Sandy complained.

"But she's so independent, Sandy. She likes to prove that she can make it on her own."

"He can be so rude," Sandy apologized to Kelly.

Kelly smiled. Jarod—oblivious to the entire conversation—warned Sandy that "Old Man Kruger" would be quizzing them on Monday on all points of the Constitution.

Dan Marquette ground the truck into gear and headed east, toward the river.

Kelly closed her eyes and leaned back in the seat, wondering what she was doing out with them. Sandy turned on the radio, and something soft and soothing came on. Kelly opened her eyes and noticed that it was a beautiful day. The sky was a soft blue, adorned with the slightest puffs of cloud, and the sun was strong and sure. It would be warm all day, no chance of rain. The river would still be cool, and it would be a perfect day for tubing.

Kelly smiled. It wasn't such a bad idea, after all. She couldn't remember the last time that she had been out just to have fun.

Eventually Dan pulled the truck off the road, and they piled out. He had five tubes in the back, big fat black tubes. Kelly watched as Dan and Jarod dug them out of the truck. She would just love to see Dan's blow a hole!

Not that it would stop him. He had that fifth tube. And the fifth tube, she discovered, was there so they could tow an ice chest along behind them. Not a bad idea, actually, she thought.

A few minutes later they were in the river. Kelly noticed that Jarod and Sandy were drifting along behind them—their hands entwined. Dan Marquette was quite relaxed, as if he'd been tubing all his life. His head was back, his feet were dangling in the water, and the extra tube was tied to his. Kelly shrugged and leaned back.

Dan took a look at the kids, then smiled at Kelly. "See? Isn't this better than sitting in your house and sulking?"

"I never sulk, Mr. Marquette," Kelly said serenely.

"Oh."

He didn't argue with her. He just pulled his second tube closer and dug into the ice chest.

"Beer, Mrs. McGraw?"

"Thank you, Mr. Marquette."

She accepted the cold beer and smiled as she sipped it, then leaned back and rested her head against her tube. The river was easy here; the current was slow, and they just drifted along in the coolness of the water, with the sun beating down upon them.

She grinned to herself. Washington city dweller. Wait until they hit the rapids! The water was a little bit low, and maneuvering over the rocks might turn out to be tricky. She couldn't wait to see how he did.

She opened her eyes and asked him sweetly, "Just what do you do for a living, Mr. Marquette?"

He shrugged. "I write: historical pieces, non-fiction."

Kelly lifted an eyebrow. "You seem to do rather well at it. I wouldn't have imagined..."

He laughed. "No, I've never had anything on the *New York Times*' bestseller list. No million sellers. But what I write doesn't change. Universities order so many a year. Most of my stuff is available in the national parks."

Kelly digested that information for a moment. "So what are you doing here?" she asked him. "For some reason, I got the impression you had been working for the Smithsonian.''

He sipped his beer and went on to tell her that he had been doing a book on early American life in Washington. He liked this area because it offered easy access to so many of the places where he had to go for his research. ''I'm working on arms right now.''

''Arms?''

''Weapons. There was a factory right outside of town, you know. And I'm researching the arsenal that brought on the whole John Brown thing. There's a gold mine of history here, you know.''

Kelly didn't answer him. She had never thought of it that way. The Harpers Ferry/Bolivar area was just home, and home had always come with fun and fascinating legends.

She suddenly found herself warming to the subject, telling him how things had changed since she'd been little, how the National Park Service had really saved the area after the numerous floods that had almost destroyed it. She told him that he would have to go on the ''ghost tour,'' that it was wonderful, and she started to list some of the books the local small press had issued that he could buy.

''You know quite a bit about the region, don't you?'' he asked her.

''West Virginia, born and bred.'' She laughed.

''Want to help me?''

''Help you what?''

''Do research. While I'm studying weapons, I might as well get into history and folklore, too.''

''Oh, I don't know,'' Kelly murmured, shying back. He reached over suddenly, and she almost gasped; he was only grabbing her empty beer can so he could toss it back into the cooler.

"Want another?"

"Oh, I don't know..."

"Well, it's really not fair if you don't pretend to get a bit drunk. I mean, where is the challenge if you're stone-cold sober?"

"Whatever are you talking about?"

He grinned. His devil's grin. A perfect grin for Daryl. "Nothing, really."

She didn't say anything else, but she suddenly had another beer in her hand.

Laughter from behind roused her, and she turned to see a group of people on a raft passing by them. They were all throwing water at each other. Someone missed and hit Sandy, who shrieked with laughter; Jarod responded by dousing the group on the raft.

Watching it all, Kelly smiled, then rested her head against the tube again. It really was fun. The beer had made her feel light—not drunk, certainly, not even tipsy, just light and able to smile easily.

Had it really been almost eighteen years since she had felt like laughing this way? With everything so easy, no pressure...

Eighteen years...

Since she and David had been like Jarod and Sandy—so young, and so in love with being in love! But they hadn't gotten much help. Her mother had been dead, and David's parents had been furious. She and David had started out with nothing, and she'd spent almost five years rushing from work to pick up Jarod and back to work. No eating out—they couldn't afford it.

Not too much time for love, either. They had both been too tired. David from his schoolwork and his part-time job; she from her nine-to-five job during the day and trying to be a loving parent in the hours that she had left. And then David had gotten out of school, and it had been her turn to start studying art.

Hard... That was all she could remember. Everything had been so hard. And then, ironically, as soon as she had finished school—another five-year span, because she hadn't been able to take as many courses each year as she should have—David had gotten into that stupid hang-gliding club and... died.

Years ago now. Almost seven years. Seven years in which everything had gone on being hard. Raising Jarod alone, worrying about the bills, wishing she had majored in something more practical than art. She'd had the talent to survive and keep them comfortable, just not quite enough to make them rich....

"A penny for them. A dime. A quarter. Hell, I'd even give you a dollar."

Kelly's eyes flew open, and she found Dan Marquette staring at her intently. A flood of heat washed over her body at his look. She knew that he could see her mind, her thoughts. Could see the way her wet T-shirt clung to her body...

"They wouldn't be worth it," she told him. And then she grinned suddenly, looking past him. The current was picking up, and they were approaching a category four rapid—one that was nice and tricky— and very likely to spill him head over heels.

"Rapid coming up," she said lightly.

He turned, saw it and nodded.

"Yes, it is."

"Hey!" Jarod called out from behind. "We're coming up on a rough one."

Kelly smiled serenely as her tube began to pick up speed. The people on the raft, she noticed, had stopped for lunch on the rocks. They had a little audience up there, an audience who had just gone over the rapids and knew how rough they were. An audience just waiting to see who would flip over!

Kelly maneuvered her tube skillfully past the rocks, loving the cool spray against her face, inhaling the fresh air. She was rocked and jolted, then rocked and jolted all over again, but she went with the flow, and eased back into the rushing current as she left the rocks behind. She heard a shriek behind her and, turning, saw that Jarod had just saved Sandy from capsizing. They were both laughing and waving to the audience up on the rocks.

Kelly looked back to Dan Marquette. He was still there, serenely sipping his beer, apparently undaunted by the rapids.

He laughed. "What's the matter, Mrs. McGraw?" he called to her. "Was I supposed to have been dashed to bits?"

"Of course not!" she retorted. "I'd hate to see you really hurt!"

"Just flogged and humiliated, huh?"

She didn't respond. She laid her head back again and let the water carry her along. It felt good. It felt so, so good! The fresh, cool, clean water, the sun against her face. The gurgle of the river and the laughter in the distance...

Suddenly her tube got snagged on a submerged branch, and she was plunged face downward into the river, with her tube flying off into the distance.

Coughing and sputtering, she came to the surface. The water wasn't deep, no more than four feet, and she ended up sprawling across a rock.

And she wasn't alone.

He was leaning over her. Tall, dark—and diabolical. His hands were resting on either side of her face, and she could feel the heat of his body.

He leaned closer, laughing. "West Virginia, born and bred, huh? You missed that branch, Mrs. Mc-Graw."

There really was no other choice. She made a frenzied swish with her hand and sent a wall of water flying up into his handsome face.

He coughed; he sputtered. And then she was lifted off the rock and dragged beneath the water. In defense she grabbed at his legs. Legs like tree trunks, muscled, wonderfully masculine, with a bevy of short, coarse dark hairs that pricked her flesh . . .

"Oh!"

She came up for air, only to find herself dragged below again, then back up, gasping. Finally she was dragged to shore and laid out flat, with the trees overhead and the sun shining through the branches and Dan Marquette stretched above her.

She was smiling, she realized. Smiling and laughing and staring into his dark eyes.

She was dying to touch him. Dying to run her fingers through his drenched dark hair, trace his bronzed features with the pads of her fingers, run her thumb over the full sensuality of his lower lip.

She inhaled sharply, and held her breath, then realized that he was staring down at her, his breath held, too. The dark flame in his eyes was the flame of desire, and the heat that emanated from his body was something like... wanting.... Something like need.

"Kelly..."

He reached out and touched her, running his thumb over her lower lip, brushing his knuckles over her throat. And, God help her, she couldn't move. Couldn't protest. Didn't want to.

Not at all. Something was growing in her. A sweet throbbing, an excitement. His breath caressed her cheek like the touch of his hand. Like his flesh against hers.

Oh, no! she thought. It was like... magic. She wanted it to go on forever, like her fantasies in *Dark of the Moon*. She wasn't of the earth, not anymore. She was on a cloud, and all she could see or feel was Dan Marquette, calling to her on levels that she had forgotten existed.

She wanted to wrap her arms around him. She wanted to press her body against him. She wanted...

"Mom! Dan! You two okay? Where are you?"

Jarod's voice broke the spell. Deftly, with an athlete's superb agility, Dan Marquette sprang to his feet and reached a hand down to Kelly. She took it, and he pulled her to her feet. Kelly felt herself flush in embarrassment.

"We're fine," Dan called out, exhaling raggedly. "We're fine. We're right here."

He looked at Kelly, who tried to look away. He caught her chin and spoke quickly, huskily. "Don't! Don't you dare try to deny it!"

"Deny what?"

His features hardened, and her heart skipped a beat. But then he smiled slowly, very slowly. "I simply won't let you," he said.

Again she couldn't reply, because Sandy and Jarod were hurrying over, and they were both laughing and acting as if nothing, absolutely nothing, was wrong.

As if the world could remain—normal.

Which it couldn't, of course. Kelly knew that her world would never, ever be the same again.

Chapter 5

They came to Dan's little "shack" at about three in the afternoon. It was really cute, a nice little frame structure right on the water, with two bedrooms, a kitchen, a living/dining area, and a river-facing patio with a barbecue. The coals were hot when they got there—Reeves, the gentleman's gentleman, had been and gone—and they were all set to go. Corn and potatoes had been left to cook; the meat, marinated, was waiting for them on a covered plate in the refrigerator.

Kelly didn't have to do anything but lie in the sun and wait. Dan stood over the barbecue, and Sandy and Jarod set the table. They talked about Harpers Ferry while they ate, Jarod telling Sandy about George Washington's interest in the place—and his investments in the Chesapeake and Ohio Canal that had made Harpers Ferry an ideal place for an armaments factory.

"Most people thought of it as a pit, nothing more," Jarod said. "But when you stand up on the cliffs and watch the Shenandoah meet the Potomac, and see Maryland, Virginia and West Virginia come together, there isn't any place more beautiful in the world!"

"Aren't you enthusiastic!" Dan teased him.

"You wait," Jarod retorted lightly. "You just haven't been here long enough."

"Hmm. Well, I will be. I'm counting on your mother to naturalize me."

Jarod gazed at Kelly curiously. Kelly gazed down at her barbecued ribs.

"That's a great idea," Jarod said.

"Really, I don't know that much," Kelly protested. "Not the exact facts and figures—"

"Facts and figures are easy to come by. Lore and legend aren't," Dan said. "Sandy, there's some fruit in the refrigerator if you want to go get it, honey. Grapes, peaches, apples. I'm going to make sure the coals are all out."

Jarod went to help Sandy—as if she couldn't carry out a bowl of fruit by herself. Kelly stretched and walked back down to the river, where they'd piled the tubes up on a little dock. She stretched out on the wood, feeling the late afternoon sun wash over her warmly.

She hesitated, thinking that she'd love to rip off her T-shirt and go for a spring tan. The sun felt so good.

She grasped the hem of the shirt and paused, thinking that she should have chosen a different bathing suit. But then, she'd wanted to look sexy when she'd put the damn thing on, hadn't she?

And now she didn't know if she had the nerve or not.

What nerve? she asked herself hotly. First he thought of her as a kid—then he tried to torment her to death! She was simply going to ignore the man.

Having made up her mind, Kelly ripped off the T-shirt and settled back comfortably. She felt the sun against her bare flesh, and it was delicious.

A second later, she started. She was no longer alone. Dan Marquette was sitting beside her, a cluster of purple grapes in his hand, a watchful grin on his features.

"Want some grapes?"

"No."

"Want to feed me some grapes?"

"No!"

He laughed and stretched out beside her. Kelly rolled over, staring out at the water, resting her chin against her knuckles.

"Just how long have you been in town?" she asked him. The area was so small that she was amazed people hadn't been talking about him. But maybe they had been; maybe she just hadn't been listening.

"Since January."

"From D.C.?"

"As of late." He popped a grape into his mouth. "We were in Colorado before. Lots and lots of white water there, Mrs. McGraw, which is why I didn't flip over when you were hoping I would."

"I wasn't hoping—"

"You were."

"Are you always this negative?"

"Only with hostile people."

"Hmph!" Kelly rolled back around and sat, hugging her knees. She grinned, proud of herself because she had overpowered the temptation to smash the grapes into his handsome face. "I didn't start out hostile. You came into my house and attacked me, and then attacked my son—"

"I was upset. Understandably so. What if Sandra had been madly in love and pregnant to boot, and Jarod had considered her nothing more than a one-night stand?"

"You should have asked first," Kelly said primly.

"Maybe I should have."

"You asked to speak with my father," Kelly reminded him.

"I can't help it if you're—"

"Short?" Kelly supplied, and he burst into laughter, rolling up to sit Indian style before her.

"Young," he said softly. She opened her mouth to protest, but he filled it with a grape. Her teeth grazed his finger, and a fire seemed to burn in some secret center of her.

She lowered her eyes, fighting it. It was absurd, the way she felt everything so strongly when she was around him.

"Why does that make you so defensive?" he demanded softly. "The rest of the world is trying mud packs and spas and healing waters and hair dyes to get where you are naturally!"

To avoid having to answer, Kelly snatched the grapes from him, took two and chewed them slowly, staring out over the water again.

He cleared his throat. "Mrs. McGraw?"

Kelly stared back at him, ready to retort sharply, but something about his appearance made her change her mind. Her heart started an erratic thumping, and she felt uncomfortably warm. She looked down at the wood of the dock.

He cared. He cared about what she had to say. He could tease mercilessly and be blunt to the point of rudeness, but in the end, she knew, from something akin to tenderness in his eyes, he really cared.

I don't want you caring about me! she thought. But then... He was sexy. He was gorgeous. He was striking. He was mature. He was single. They already shared a certain relationship....

She inhaled sharply. Yes, they shared a relationship. Her son had gotten Dan's daughter pregnant.

She shouldn't get any closer to Dan Marquette. This whole thing was so delicate and tenuous. For Sandra's sake, for Jarod's sake, she needed to be mature and objective.

And Dan Marquette...

Dan Marquette knew how to date. He knew how to laugh, and how to play, how to say the right things. Kelly knew—she just knew!—that he'd enjoyed umpteen affairs since his marriage had ended, and that he had walked away from every one of them unscathed. She didn't mean to judge him; he had spoken casually of his wife's desertion, but it must have been the biggest hurt of his life. She hadn't just deserted him—she had deserted Sandy. But that had been years ago. He was a big boy, playing the major league.

And Kelly didn't know how to play at all. She'd always been too busy. Too occupied with just getting by to learn how to date, how to meet a man, how to flirt—how to do anything! And this didn't seem like a very good time to learn.

She stood up quickly, uncomfortably. "We really have to be getting home," she murmured.

He remained on the dock for several moments. Several long moments, during which he watched her.

Kelly felt his eyes. Felt them rake over her. Felt them fill her with warmth until she flushed.

But then he, too, rose smoothly, without a word. "Whatever you say, Mrs. McGraw."

Kelly cast the grape stem into the river and watched it float away. Dan turned and called to Sandra and Jarod, and then he strode back to the barbecue to make sure that the coals were out.

They didn't go back in the tubes. Kelly was finally able to meet Reeves when that very proper and very polite gray-haired old gentleman came to pick them up in Dan's car.

She didn't even have to talk to Dan again. He had Reeves drop him off at the truck, then drive the others home.

Don't do it! Don't do it!

Dan kept repeating the words to himself, but they didn't change anything. He looped his tie and secured it, moving mechanically, not really seeing himself.

Well, he was dressed. And more fashionably than he usually was, too. More formally. Jacket, tie, vest. Hell, there was nowhere in Bolivar or Harpers Ferry where you needed to be that dressed up. Maybe in Charleston...

But he didn't want to go into Charleston. He wanted to pick her up and take her to the Hilltop House and have dinner. And when dinner was over he wanted to walk outside. To let nightfall find them where they could look down on the river and up over to Maryland Heights and to the horizon, where land and water and sky all met with a beauty that was gentle and serene and breathtaking.

She won't even come with you, friend! he warned himself. He hadn't called her, and he didn't intend to—he was still trying to convince himself that seeing her at all wouldn't be a very big mistake. It was amazing that things were going as well as they were. Amazing that Sandra and Jarod were taking things in stride. Amazing that he and Kelly McGraw were managing to take a helpful and active interest in the children's future.

Don't blow that! he cautioned himself.

But the warnings just weren't any good. He wasn't sure when it had begun, the fascination—the obsession! He had to get to know her. Had to learn what made her move and function and tick . . .

He groaned aloud softly and readjusted his tie.

Find another woman!

But he didn't want to find another woman. He wanted this one. He'd loved the sparks and blue fire in her eyes when she'd fought him that first day, like a little tigress, fierce in battle, determined to let no harm come to her cub. He'd thought her a child that first day. Now, of course, he knew that she was anything but.

He never should have taken her tubing. Never should have seen her in that soaking wet T-shirt over that minimal bathing suit. Never should have studied the delicate lines of her face when her hair had been drenched and pulled back, revealing her features so cleanly.

He never should have watched that flowing wealth of golden hair dry over her shoulders, curl over her breasts. . . .

No, she wasn't a child. Not at all!

But she was almost as innocent as one, he knew. Mature, fierce, responsible—but innocent as all damn hell, and here he was . . .

"I'm just going to ask her to dinner!"

"What was that, sir?"

Dan didn't know that he had spoken aloud until Reeves Remington cleared his throat and asked the question.

Dan turned ruefully away from the hallway mirror and grinned at Reeves. "What did you think of Mrs. McGraw, Reeves?"

Reeves cleared his throat again, dusting an imaginary speck of lint from his impeccable white shirt. "I think that she's quite . . . charming."

"Charming is *not* what you were going to say," Dan told him dryly. Reeves had been with him for almost eighteen years. He knew the elegant old man better than he had ever known his own father, and there had been definite disapproval in Reeves' voice.

"Young."

Dan nodded slowly. "She'd not that young, Reeves. Her son is about to marry my daughter."

"And a very nice young man he is!" Reeves said enthusiastically.

"Ah." Dan leaned against the sideboard and grinned. "Jarod is a nice young man. He seduced my nice, innocent young daughter, but he's okay. And Mrs. McGraw is 'charming' and 'young.' So what you're attempting to say here—"

Reeves stiffened very regally. "I never attempt to say, sir! You're demanding an opinion, I'll give you one! She's too innocent, too charming, and too young for you!"

"Hey! I wasn't demanding an opinion that vigorously!" Dan protested, laughing.

"Well," Reeves murmured, "it's true."

"It probably is," Dan said unhappily.

"Shall I put the car back into the garage?" Reeves asked hopefully.

Dan shook his head. "No."

"You're still going out with her?"

"Oh, for heaven's sake, Reeves! I'm asking her out to dinner!"

"Not to make love on the mountain, huh, Dad?"

Dan spun around in startled surprise to see Sandy, her chin perched on her hand, her elbow on the banister, as she stared down at him with vast amusement.

He arched a disapproving brow. "Young lady—"

"Dad, I'm just kidding!"

"Sandy, don't you dare talk about...things like that to me. I'm still not accustomed to the fact that you're going to have a baby. Honestly, young woman—"

"Whoa, please forgive me, Dad!" she pleaded, running down the stairs to throw herself against him. "I'm sorry. Honest! I just couldn't help it! Reeves was standing there staring at you, looking so grim. Dad?"

He held her away from him and stared at her with narrowed eyes, then kissed her forehead. "Sandra Marquette, just don't you dare come to me—"

"Okay! Okay!" She didn't sound duly chastised, though; in fact, she was laughing. She smoothed his lapels and inhaled deeply. "But you do smell great. And I love the suit. You're devastating. Isn't he, Reeves?"

"Oh, yes, miss. Just devastating!" Reeves sniffed.

Dad groaned softly again. "Good night, Reeves. Good night, Sandy."

" 'Night, Dad.''

He paused at the door, turned back and looked inquiringly at his daughter. "What are you up to this evening?"

"Jarod is coming over."

"Oh?"

"I shall be here the entire time, Mr. Marquette," Reeves said primly. "I shall make them popcorn, and they can watch the TV, and that, young lady, will be that!"

Sandy lowered her eyes, but Dan knew she was smiling. He knew, too, that she loved Reeves and would be very good with him as her chaperon.

Where were you three months ago? he wondered. Where were you when she met this boy? But he just shook his head and started out the door again. What was done was done. It seemed inconceivable that the two youngsters who were about to have a popcorn party were going to be newlyweds and parents sooner than any of them wanted to think.

"So what the hell am I doing?" he asked himself again as he sat behind the steering wheel.

Messing everything up....

But, none of his arguments held any weight. He gunned the engine, and started for the McGraw house.

It was just going to be dinner.

"There's no game tonight?" Kelly called over her shoulder to Jarod. He was stalking around the house bare-chested, wearing a pair of jeans and waiting for his favorite shirt to go through the dryer. Kelly was perched on her stool, staring blankly at an equally blank piece of paper. Thank God she didn't have an imminent deadline. She wouldn't make it. She had told herself that she was going to sit down and work, and she had managed the sitting down part, but the work was coming very, very slowly.

Jarod came up behind her and kissed the top of her head. "Mom, I told you, the game is tomorrow night. There's nothing going on. I'm going over to Sandy's, and we're going to watch television."

As he started out of the room, Kelly swung around on her stool. "Just television?"

"Just television."

"Is her dad going to be there?"

"I don't know, Mom," Jarod said with forced patience, "but don't worry, we won't have too much fun. Not the kind of fun that you're worrying about. Not that I can see what difference it would make at this point—"

"Jarod!"

He grinned. "Reeves is going to be there."

"Oh?"

Jarod laughed. "Mom, could *you* fool around with Reeves there?"

Kelly turned back to her blank piece of paper. "I'm not a high school senior," she reminded her son.

He snapped his fingers. "Oh, that's right. I forgot! You forgot how to fool around years ago!"

"Jarod!"

Kelly swung around again in a fury—to no avail. Jarod had dropped his bombshell and hastily left the room. "Kids!" she muttered out loud, then bit her lip. Maybe she could do her strip this month on a problem between parents and kids.

The doorbell started to ring just as Kelly brought her pencil down to the paper. "Jarod! Get that, will you?" she called.

But Jarod didn't get it; with a sigh, Kelly decided that he must have gone down to the basement to get his shirt. She slid off her stool and went to the door, then stepped back, feeling overawed, when Dan Marquette stepped in.

"Hi."

"Hi."

"What are you doing?"

"Working." Kelly held up her pencil for him to see.

He smiled and took the pencil out of her fingers. "I need some help. Want to go to dinner with me?"

Kelly swallowed. She did want to go to dinner. She was dying to leave the house, because she wasn't in any mood for work. And the way he looked, she would love to go anywhere with him. Anywhere at all. If he had stepped in and said, "Hi, want to have an affair?" she would have been ready to nod and go running off with him.

Are you losing your mind? she screamed inwardly. Maybe she was. The fabric of his suit made her long to reach out and touch him, just as she wanted to reach up and touch his dark hair, still damp from his shower. Touch his cheeks, freshly shaven . . .

"Hi, Dan!" Jarod, pulling on his shirt, had made an appearance in the hallway.

"Hi, Jarod."

"You're not at home," Jarod blurted.

Dan grinned. "No, I'm not. But Reeves is."

Jarod looked at the floor, blushing. "I know." Then he looked at Dan curiously. "What are you, umm, doing here?"

"I came to see if your mom wanted to go up to the Hilltop House for dinner."

"Oh."

Jarod looked curiously at his mother, who refused to meet his eyes.

"I'd have to shower and change," she murmured.

Dan shrugged. "Whenever you're ready."

Kelly nodded vaguely and started up the stairs. Jarod watched her and stared at Dan.

"Dinner?"

Dan laughed. "Dinner."

"Yeah, well, Reeves won't be with the two of you if he's with the two of us."

"That's right."

Jarod started to laugh. "All right, all right! But..." His laughter faded; he felt extremely awkward. "Be, uh, decent. Be good, I mean. I, uh, I mean..."

"Dinner, Jarod," Dan said very softly. "We're just going to dinner."

"Yeah. Well, I'm, uh, on my way, I guess. Can I get you something while you're waiting? A beer? Scotch? Glass of wine?"

"A beer would be nice."

Jarod nodded and headed for the kitchen. Dan was still in the hallway when he returned. "Uh, why don't you have a seat in the parlor," he suggested. "Mom won't be long. She's quick. She's real quick. She's not a primper. You know how some women are—an hour and a half in the shower and all that. Fifty minutes for lipstick and mascara. Mom's not like that. She's quick. Oh boy, yes, she's real quick. You won't have to wait but a minute."

"Jarod..."

"You can make yourself comfortable right here. In the parlor."

"Jarod..."

"Well, I guess I'll be going. Sandy is expecting me."

"Yes."

"You drove over here, right? Yeah, of course, you drove. I was going to use my mother's car. That's still okay, huh? I mean, you've got your car, so you won't be needing hers. You will be using your car, though, right? You won't be staying here alone, will you?"

"No. We'll be using my car. If you were planning on taking your mother's car, I'm sure that's still fine."

"Yeah." Jarod backed toward the door. "Yeah. Well, have a nice dinner. Have a good time, huh?"

Dan nodded. "Thanks, I'm sure we will. You, too."

Jarod went out the front door and closed it behind him. Dan stared after him, a secretive smile on his face.

"Well, you know what it feels like now, huh, young man?" And he laughed softly. No, Jarod couldn't really know what if felt like. Not yet. He would have to wait until he had a daughter of his own.

Which might be quite soon, Dan reflected dryly. He picked up a magazine off the sideboard in the hallway and walked into the parlor with it. He hesitated, glancing toward the stairs. I'm going to go straight into the parlor and wait for your mother, Jarod, he promised silently. I'm going to sit here like the perfect gentleman...."

But at that very moment there was a piercing scream of terror and panic. A woman's scream—Kelly's scream—coming from upstairs.

Dan dropped both the magazine and his beer and bolted up the stairs.

Kelly had been quick. She'd always assumed that she could get ready quickly because there wasn't that much of her to do anything with. Her hair was long, her makeup light. If she had something more to do something with, she reasoned, she would probably take longer.

As it was, she hadn't really thought—not about herself, not about the evening ahead. She had quickly thrown open her closet door and gazed at her clothing. She didn't need anything terribly formal, though he did look awfully nice in his three-piece suit. The vest was the killer. The way it fit. Or maybe it was the jacket.

Or maybe his clothes had nothing to do with any of it. Maybe it was the warm, mahogany of his eyes, or the laughter in them, or maybe the slightly crooked slant of his smile.

Kelly had realized that she was just standing in front of the closet, smiling stupidly. She'd reached into the closet for a light blue silk dress. It was a halter-type garment, strapless, with a full skirt that swayed and swirled when she walked. The dress was casual, but it felt elegant because of the material. Nothing felt as soft and slinky and sexy as silk.

Humming, she had laid the dress out on the bed, then delved into her drawer for panties and stockings, and headed for the bathroom. She'd pulled back the curtain to start the water and frowned slightly, thinking that she needed to remember to open the bathroom window after her shower. The tile was molding because she never remembered to open the window.

Kelly hesitated, then went ahead and opened it. Who could possibly look through her bathroom window? Her neighbors were hundreds of yards away through the trees.

She opened the window and started to hum again, forgetting all about it. She was trying to forget about everything, in fact. After all, if she thought about it, she was on the way to making a grave mistake. She was falling for the man who was going to be Jarod's father-in-law. The complications were endless.

No, she told herself. She wasn't falling for him....

But she was, and she knew it. The attraction had been instant. Men like Dan Marquette just didn't come along every day. She hadn't dated much before, and she hadn't fallen for anyone because she simply hadn't met anyone who was anything like Dan Marquette before.

Kelly sudsed herself and set her face beneath the spray. Don't think! she reminded herself. If you think too long, you'll remember all the reasons why you shouldn't be going! You'll remember how you felt, warm and hot and nearly delirious, when he bent over you. When he touched your lips...

It was no big thing!

It was everything. I wanted to kiss him, she admitted silently. I wanted to run my fingers through his hair, and rub my palms over his back, and...

She turned around, letting the water sluice through her hair, and as she opened her eyes, she screamed.

Someone was staring in at her. Someone who was two flights up from street level, just beyond the bathroom window, staring in at her.

"Kelly!"

She couldn't breathe; she couldn't gasp out a reply. She could only stand with the water sluicing over her. She wasn't a coward, she told herself. She was short, but not a coward. It was just the absolute terror of looking out and seeing two beady little eyes staring in at her. Staring and staring, golden and glowing.

"Kelly!"

She dimly heard the bathroom door crash open; then the curtain was ripped back. The water was still running, and she was still standing there in nothing but her birthday suit.

Dan Marquette was standing there, too. Tense, anxious, concerned, ready to do battle. Just like the knights in her fantasy kingdom, ready to do battle against the creatures of the darkness.

And the eyes... The eyes were still there. Kelly, too stunned to recognize her state of undress, pointed toward them.

Marquette looked, then he looked back at her. In a panic, Kelly threw herself against him. All of her. Dripping wet.

"Didn't you see them! Oh, my God, Dan! Didn't you see them?"

"See what, Kelly?"

"The eyes! You must have seen them! Those eyes, staring in!"

He was holding her. All of her. He had thought the sight of her in her bathing suit had been heaven, but this...

This was paradise. If he had been Adam and Kelly had been Eve, he would have prayed for original sin to begin.

She was perfect! Smooth and sleek and quivering in his arms. Her flesh was softer than silk; she was warmer than warm, she was...

"Didn't you see them?"

Her eyes...

They were too marvelous to be simply blue. No color was that bright. That wonderful.

"Dan!"

"Eyes?"

"Dan, there were eyes! Staring at me!"

"What? Eyes? Oh, yes. I—oh!"

He grabbed her towel from the rack and handed it to her quickly. "I'll go check," he promised her.

"Dan, be careful! There's someone out there! Oh, God, Dan, be careful!"

Be careful.... She was worried, he thought. She thought that he might be in danger.

Oh, Kelly, he thought. The danger wasn't outside; it didn't matter who or what those eyes belonged to. The danger was inside.

The danger was seeing her, touching her, holding her.

The danger was when he returned!

Chapter 6

Kelly managed to wrap the towel that Dan had handed her around herself, but that was as far as she got. She stood there shivering, thinking that she should move, but unable to do so. Even though the eyes were gone, they were still ingrained in her memory along with all the horror she had felt.

Seconds ticked by, then minutes. The fear slowly began to ease from her, and a deep sense of shame set in. What must he think of her? Screaming her head off, jumping—dripping wet and naked—into his arms.

What was going on down there? Why didn't he come back? Was everything all right? Maybe she should be calling the police. Maybe she had sent him out to meet some horrible danger.

No, this was a quiet neighborhood. Nothing was going to happen to him.

But where was he?

Kelly forced herself to step back into the tub. She steeled herself to go to the window, to look out. Someone was there, standing by the big oak.

"Dan?"

He looked up at the sound of her voice. "Kelly, I can't find anything. Whoever or whatever was here is gone now. I'm coming up."

She nodded, staring down at him, but she didn't move.

A moment later she was frantically asking herself what was wrong with her, because he was back in the steaming bathroom and she was still standing in the tub with nothing but a towel between them.

And then, absurdly, she decided that it didn't matter. It wouldn't have mattered if she had been wearing armor from head to toe. Nothing could be a real barrier between them. Not clothing, not time, not place, not situation.

Kelly McGraw, you don't know this man very well, she warned herself. It's wrong.

"You—you couldn't find anything?" she managed to ask him. Her voice was quivering.

And it should quiver, of course. She had been frightened. But she wasn't frightened now, not with him standing beside her. Her voice wasn't quivering from fear. It was quivering because she could feel his eyes on her. She'd never seen darker eyes. Or brighter ones. They were deep, dark, fascinating, wicked and diabolical, both threatening and promising mischief, never malice. Ecstasy....

He cleared his throat. "There are some broken branches. Someone or something did come up the tree. But it—he?—is gone now."

His eyes never left her face, but his gaze was like a caress. He stood so still, so tall, filling the room. She could smell his after-shave, and she could almost feel the rasp of his coat against her skin.

He cleared his throat—again. "Are you all right?"

Kelly nodded.

What did he really mean? Or did it matter? None of their words meant anything at all. She should be embarrassed. She should excuse herself and run into the bedroom to hide. She should be grasping for her clothes, but instead she felt the soft beginning of a smile curving her mouth.

"Should I get you anything?" he asked. "A drink? Some brandy?"

Me? he added silently. All of me. You'll never be afraid again. I won't let you; I swear it.

He should leave, of course. He shouldn't be standing here in her bathroom. The danger was gone. He'd performed correctly. She'd screamed; he'd rushed in. The danger, whatever it had been, was gone now.

Gone—or just beginning?

Water clung to her in delightful droplets. Her hair was drying in soft golden wisps. The towel wasn't really around her; it was just kind of against her. Against her breasts. She looked soft. So soft. Tiny, delicate, exquisite, like a china figurine.

But she wouldn't be breakable. . . .

His smile curved slowly, in answer to her own. He saw the pattern on the walls. Kelly's towel, soft brown with an elaborate monogrammed *M*.

He took a step toward her, and she didn't move, so he took another step, then lifted her over the bathtub rim and against him. He felt the tremendous shivering that seized her body. She didn't look away from him. She tilted her head back, and her eyes met his. He could have sworn that his heart stopped. Actually stopped. He brushed his knuckles over her cheek, then held her face carefully between his palms.

"I promised your son that we'd go to dinner," he told her.

"We will go to dinner," she promised.

He bent down and kissed her. Kissed her with all the yearning in his heart and soul. His tongue slid over her lips, grazing against her teeth, plunging and delving into her sweet hot depths. His fingers tangled in her hair, those damp, golden strands. He felt her nape with his fingers, her shoulder blades, the smooth length of her back. She was soft... softer than anything he had known. Her flesh tempted and seduced him. He felt for a moment how very small she was, and he shuddered, but when he thought that he should draw back, she pressed herself more closely against him.

The towel slid from between them. She was kissing him back now. Her tongue, a sweet torment, was deep in his mouth; her fingers were entwined in the hair at his nape. They merged together in that kiss, and the night stopped. Time ceased to be. When they finally pulled apart, neither of them could breathe, and neither of them cared. He saw only her beautiful eyes, blue and open and honest, searing into his own.

"Oh, Kelly," he whispered , and then he kissed her again. When he drew away this time, there was nothing left to say, nothing that needed to be said. What was happening between them was so right that it couldn't be denied.

"Oh, Kelly," he whispered again, and he buried his face against her throat, against the sweet damp scent of her soap, and when he moved again, it was to sweep her naked body into his arms, the only natural thing to do.

Her arms wound around him; her eyes, eternally blue, remained locked with his. Her fingers stroked his nape, and he was dimly aware that he was shaking. He had never wanted anyone as he wanted her now. She was an aching in his soul, a yearning in his heart. She compounded his desire with her own, and she made the experience transcend anything that he had ever known before.

He barely knew the way, yet his footsteps led him surely to her bed. He laid her on it, but when he tried to draw away to undress, she parted her lips and smiled, and pulled him into a kiss again.

He kicked his shoes off, far more anxious than graceful, and when the kiss ended, he was above her. Her smile, mercury and stardust, met him, and their eyes remained locked as he removed his tie, as she eased away his jacket, and they fumbled with the buttons on his shirt and vest together.

Things went in every direction. His vest to the left, his shirt to the right, his belt to the foot of the bed.

Only then did her fingers falter. He didn't urge her to go on, afraid that the magic would be broken. He stood and shed his trousers and briefs, then fell down beside her again. For a long moment they remained that way, close, barely touching, feeling the marvel of their bodies meeting.

When he moved, it was slowly. He brought his fingers against her arm, stroking languidly, tantalizingly. There was so much to savor in just that touch. The moon was out, and he could see her, could see every exotic curve and plane.

She made a little sound and moved against him, and suddenly the world was filled with brilliant color. He burned with desire. It raged within him, controlling him, and there was nothing languid about his touch when he swept his arms around her and felt the liquid motion of her body beneath his. Too fast, he warned himself. Too fast. They had just met, and he couldn't let passion take control.

But it had.

A hoarse, guttural cry escaped him, and he shifted his weight over hers. He let his trembling hand roam free over her breast, then touched that seductive flesh with his kiss, with his tongue, holding her nipple within his mouth, warning himself to slow down, ignoring that warning as her body arched against his.

Kelly decided that she had gone mad. But she deserved to be mad, she told herself. She was an adult; she was mature and capable and responsible.... And this was paradise!

Each time his tongue rasped against her flesh, each time she felt the deliciously callused tips of his fingers against her skin, she found paradise all over again. This was new. Entirely new. Once she had thought herself a decent lover. She had loved her husband, and life had been good.

But this... this was new. This was so intense that it was painful. So delicious that denial would be akin to death. This was something that she had never known.

She whispered his name out loud, harshly, hoarsely. His teeth were grazing her nipple while his fingers stroked the soft inner flesh of her upper thigh, and she seemed to become liquid, hot and molten. She emitted a small sound, and then a louder one, and then a searing cry as his touch probed within her, deep within her. The sensation electrified her, and she shuddered because it felt so good, so intense.

He told her to open her eyes, and she did. She stared at him with wonder, fascinated by the strength in the muscles beneath her fingers, enchanted with the passion she could read on his face. He shifted again, smiling, entering her, and she cried out boldly. For a moment she was horrified at the sound, but he laughed with such triumph and pleasure that she buried her face against his shoulder and wrapped her arms around his back.

She savored each second, each movement, each slow, subtle thrust that brought him deeper and deeper into her, made him more and more a part of her.

Her blood seemed to sing in her ears, her entire body moved to the music, his touch. She flew, and she soared, and she sobbed, because she had to reach the pinnacle, yet he held her back again and again, so that she was forced to fly and soar again.

Finally she reached it: a moment so high, so wonderful, so good, that light had never been so explosive, color had never been so brilliant. She felt as if the stars were colliding inside her, yet she knew that she was completely of the earth. As she drifted downward she smiled, because once again she could hear her breath and his, hear her heartbeat and his. Feel her flesh, damp and slick, against his.

Dan rose up on an elbow, watching her eyes again and praying that remorse wouldn't set in. It would be so easy for her to hate him now. Easy for her to feel that he had taken advantage of her, of the situation.

She smiled.

She reached up and smoothed the hair back from his forehead, ran her fingers over his cheek. He caught her hand and kissed her fingers.

"I think I'm in love," Kelly murmured.

Then she did suffer a pang of remorse. What an asinine thing to say! Wouldn't she ever grow up? Anyone with any sense knew that love and love*making* weren't the same, that a man might well run if such words were spoken too early.

But he didn't run. He grinned. Slowly. His diabolical, Daryl the Devilish Dragon grin. And he kissed her forehead.

"Kelly, do you have any idea how beautiful, how sweet, how fresh, how wonderful you are?"

She colored and curled against his chest, fingering the damp curls of dark hair there, thinking that he was beautiful. He was in wonderful shape, his muscles powerful and fascinating.

"Really?" she whispered.

"Really," he told her.

He slipped his arms around her and held her close. "What do you think that the kids are going to say?" he asked.

Kelly frowned, then sat up, laughed and straddled him. It was a wonderful feeling, natural and easy. "Actually," she told him, her eyes sparkling, "I had no intention of telling them."

He nodded. "Well," he said consideringly. And then laughed. "Well, I hadn't intended on giving them—what were Jarod's words?—a 'blow-by-blow' description, either. But they are going to realize that we're getting along much better."

"Are we?"

"I thought we got along just splendidly," he said, his dark eyes alive with sensual fire. "If you've forgotten already, I can refresh your memory."

She smiled and leaned against his chest. "I'm still not so terribly sure that we get along."

"Maybe not. Maybe only time will tell. Are you going to give me that time, Kelly?"

"Of course," she murmured. "I wouldn't have—I mean we wouldn't be here, if I didn't plan. I mean—"

Dan interrupted her, laughing, kissing her quickly. "Aha! You mean that it wasn't the moon? I didn't seduce you? You didn't run to me in terror because of the eyes in the darkness?"

Kelly withdrew slightly, watching him through narrowed eyes. "Why?"

"Why?"

"Why did you say that?"

He shook his head ruefully, hoping that he hadn't lost her because of his careless words. "No reason. I was just teasing, I suppose. Or maybe..." He paused, then took a deep breath and plunged ahead. "Maybe I wanted it to be something lasting. Maybe I don't want to call you tomorrow and have you pretend that nothing happened."

Kelly stretched out beside him, idly running her fingers over his torso. Her? Pretend that nothing had happened? He didn't know her very well. But of course that was true. They really didn't know each other at all.

Time would change that, he told her. If she gave him that time.

"Mr. Marquette," she murmured primly, "when I woke up this morning, I most certainly did not intend to spend the evening in bed with you. I didn't intend to spend the evening in bed with anyone. But having ended up here with you, I can say that I did it with open eyes. Well, once we made the...connection, that is. Oh, that still doesn't sound right, does it?''

Grinning, Dan said, "It sounds divine, Mrs. Mc-Graw. Divine."

He leaned down to kiss her. Afterward, she stared up at him breathlessly.

"Dinner," she murmured.

"Yes, I did come to take you out to dinner, didn't I?"

Kelly nodded solemnly. "And I simply can't imagine having to explain to Jarod that we never got to dinner."

"Neither can I."

He kept smiling down at her.

"Dan, if we're going to make dinner, you're going to have to move. I couldn't budge you to save my life."

"Pity," he teased.

"I'm going to have to shower all over again."

"So will I."

"So?" Excited, laughing, Kelly stared up at him. He shook his head, frowning.

"If we're going to have to go through all that, showering, dressing, I think we should make it worth-while. And I need to stack up a little time in my favor—numbers, you know."

"Numbers?"

"Hmm. As in more than once. When you wake up tomorrow morning, I want you to think not of the man with whom you made love once, but of the man with whom you made love again and again and again...."

He bent down to kiss her. Kelly raised her arm over his shoulder and read her watch.

"Hey!" she protested—when she could breathe again. "You're forgetting, dinner comes early around here! If we don't eat soon..."

Dan rose far enough above her to glance at her clock and frown. He shrugged. "We can always drive over to Charleston. It's not really that late." He smiled at her, lowering himself against her. "We've got plenty of time," he told her.

And she didn't protest.

Twenty minutes later they were in the shower—with the window closed. Kelly had decided that she would much rather live with mildew and mold than eyes that stared in at her. Especially now...

But when he made an openly amorous move with the soap, she shoved at his chest and hopped out of his way, pointing at her watch.

"We really will miss dinner!" she told him. "I keep telling you, this isn't New York or D.C. It isn't even Charleston. Things close early here!"

He laughed and agreed and remembered that he had wanted to go to the Hilltop House because they could walk after dinner and take advantage of the beautiful view.

"If you can dress in five minutes," Kelly warned him, throwing a towel his way, "we can still make it."

"I can dress in five minutes, but can you?" Dan retorted.

"I can beat you hands down, Mr. Marquette."

"Do you think so?"

"Hmm. And what are you grinning at?"

"Nothing," he assured her, drying quickly, watching her every movement, then catching her briefly when she tried to slip into her dress.

"I'm not so sure about putting my clothes on, but I can guarantee that I could get yours off in way less than five minutes."

"But you're supposed to be getting yours on! Behave!" Kelly wailed. "Honestly, if we're not in the dining room before the last sitting begins, we won't get to eat!"

He could dress in less than five minutes and so could she—they both proved it. Dan protested that Kelly's hair was still wet, but she assured him that it would dry in the car. Laughing, they ran huffing and puffing from the parking lot. They managed to get into the dining room just in time, and get seats right next to the window, too. Friday night dinner was a buffet, and their waitress, a girl Kelly had known for ages, warned them that they'd better get their food quickly, before the chef began to put things away.

Kelly piled her plate high, and Dan grinned and commented that for such a tiny creature, she could pack it away. She made a face at him and said her appetite was entirely his fault.

He didn't protest.

They didn't speak much until they had eaten, and then they both laughed again, because they had been so hungry. Kelly ordered a coffee liqueur and Dan ordered a black Irish coffee when they had finished the meal. Only then did his fingers fall over hers where they lay on the table, and only then did she smile a little awkwardly in return. The night was exquisite, as if Dan had been able to order it in advance. It wasn't light, but it wasn't completely dark. An echo of the sun remained in the sky, while the moon and the stars moved out, and a haze fell, tinted mauve and crimson.

"You know," Dan said lightly to Kelly, "Sandy is crazy about you. I'll never be able to thank you enough for that. I've been pretty good at playing two roles most of her life—but mother of the pregnant bride-to-be was something I know I couldn't have managed the way you have. Thank you. Thank you very much."

Kelly felt a pink flush suffuse her cheeks, and she wondered how on earth she could still blush so easily around him. She lifted her glass to him. "She's a beautiful girl, and you know it."

"Yeah, she is," Dan agreed, then he frowned. "You know, they both have to start making some decisions soon. This year will end; they have to decide on a college they can both go to."

Kelly shrugged. "Jarod wanted Georgetown. He wants to be a politician eventually."

"Sandy wanted the University of Miami. Premed."

"Well, they're going to have to compromise."

"Yes, they are."

"And they probably should—" Kelly broke off, hesitating.

"Should what?"

"Well, I was thinking that Georgetown would be the better choice. Don't you think that it would be smart for them to be near us?"

Kelly drew her fingers back, watching as his lashes quickly hid the thoughts that might have been betrayed in his eyes. What was he thinking? she wondered. That she was on Jarod's side—and against Sandy?

"You might be right," he said lightly.

"And they're both going to have to work," Kelly said sharply.

He shrugged. "It might not be necessary."

"What! Not necessary!"

"Kelly, damn it, I can help them."

"You'll wind up helping them straight into the ground! Dan, I want to help them, too, but they can't shirk everything. Jarod was going to have to work one way or another, and work isn't a bad thing!"

"No, it's not, but I'll be damned if Sandra is going to work for four years to put Jarod through college so he can start making a great income and divorce her!"

Kelly stared at him indignantly, then burst into laughter. "There's got to be a compromise here. Really."

"There probably is," Dan murmured, and he moved his thumb over her palm in such a way that Kelly caught her breath.

"We can't live for them—" he began, but before he could go any further, they were suddenly interrupted by a sweet, feminine voice.

"Kelly! Kelly McGraw! How good to see you, darling!"

Kelly swung around, feeling only the slightest dismay. The woman coming toward them was a very pretty natural redhead. She was exactly Kelly's own age—and in fact had known her—though not always liked her—since high school.

She was also sophisticated and elegant—and tall. Kelly wasn't at all sure that this was a night when she wanted to see her, no matter how long they had known each other.

Dan was already politely on his feet. Kelly stood, too, then wished that she had remained sitting. She felt ridiculously short. She quickly introduced her friend to Dan.

"Dan Marquette, June DeMarco. June, Dan Marq—"

"Marquette, yes, I know," June said serenely, smiling brilliantly and pulling up a chair to join them, even before Dan had a chance to help her.

June grinned at Kelly. "Mr. Marquette is the talk of the town, Kelly, you didn't know?"

"I haven't been in town enough lately, I guess," Kelly replied.

"And you know each other?"

"Our children are engaged," Dan supplied.

June's eyebrows shot up. "Kelly! You didn't tell me!"

"June, honestly, I haven't had a chance," Kelly said helplessly, but June wasn't really listening anyway. She had linked a long arm through Dan's and was telling him that she ran a simply wonderful antique shop down in the historic section. "Just a hop, a skip and a jump from the Park, where I understand you spend an awful lot of time. You really must come by!"

"I'm sure I will," Dan said noncommittally, furrowing his brows at Kelly over the rim of his cup.

Kelly laughed. "Down, June! Down. Dan, forgive her. She's only been divorced for two years, and we're still trying to teach her proper behavior."

"Oh, nuts to you, Kelly McGraw!" June teased back. She smiled at Dan. "We've been trying to teach

Kelly that widowhood does not mean instant membership in the nunnery!''

Dan choked on his coffee. Kelly reddened and quickly asked June how her daughter was doing with her ballet classes.

A minute later June admitted that she had come with a date. She beckoned him over and introduced him as Donald Milligan, an insurance broker from Sharpsburg. Donald sat down, and their waitress brought them another round of drinks.

They talked for a while about casual things; then June suddenly frowned and asked Dan, "Your daughter isn't home alone, is she?"

Dan shook his head. "No. Jarod is over there, for one," he laughed wryly. "And we have a man named Reeves—sort of a butler, sort of an old friend—who lives with us. Why?"

"Why?" June sounded concerned, and she stared at Kelly uneasily. "Haven't you heard?"

"Heard what?"

"The police, the sheriff's office and even the FBI are after an escaped Tennessee convict. He's called the Peeper. He was convicted of thirteen assaults! You haven't heard? You didn't watch the news?"

Kelly gasped and stared at Dan, ashen and dismayed. "The Peeper!" she nearly shrieked.

"Calm down, Kelly, you don't know for sure. It might have been a raccoon or a—"

"What might have been a raccoon?" June demanded.

"Kelly thought that someone was watching her tonight," Dan said carefully.

"Thought!" Kelly exclaimed. "I didn't 'think' anything! I saw those eyes staring in at me!"

"My, my," Donald Milligan said unhappily. "What a shame that you didn't call the police."

"Thank goodness Dan was with you," June purred.

"Yes, thank goodness," Dan murmured.

Donald said that Kelly should call the police anyway, and she did, from the inn. Dan spoke to them, too, and then, since the dining room had closed, they all walked out to look at the view. After a little more conversation they split up and went to their respective cars.

Kelly hugged her arms to her chest uneasily.

"You're not staying home tonight," Dan said bluntly.

"What?" She looked up at him, confused.

"You're not staying home alone."

"But I won't be alone! I have a son who's barely an inch shorter than you are!"

"Kelly, the police made it sound as if this man is really dangerous. Kelly, to think that it might have been him, right outside your house..."

She shuddered, willing to rest against him. "Thank God you were there. And to think, we were so mesmerized by each other that we didn't even worry... Oh, my God! If you hadn't been there...! Jarod wasn't there then, either!"

"That does it!" Dan stated flatly, gripping her elbow and pulling her along. "You are staying at my house."

"I can't! What—"

"You'll stay, and Jarod will stay."

"Oh, that's just great! The kids will adore that!" Kelly blurted out sarcastically.

"Kelly!" Exasperatedly Dan pushed back a straying lock of hair from his forehead. "Not together. You

can have your own room, and so can he. My house is
enormous. We'll tell the kids what happened—"

"We will not!" Kelly yelped.

"Not that!" Dan retorted. "We'll tell them about
the Peeper, and the eyes staring in at you. That's all.
Hey, they'll get to see what they look like when they
wake up in the morning. That knowledge just might
help make their marriage work."

"Cynic!" Kelly charged.

"I have a right to be," he told her dryly.

"I don't know, Dan," Kelly began.

"I do," he said, and he said it in such a superior
tone that she was tempted to argue.

But she was a little bit frightened, too, so she didn't.
She stared straight ahead and thought of his face
plastered on her mythical dragon.

He started laughing suddenly, glancing her way.

"What?" she demanded.

"We get to see each other first thing in the morning, too."

"I'm absolutely glamorous," she retorted.

To her amazement, he reached out and dragged her
close to his side. "I'll bet you are, darling. I'll just bet
you are."

"Still short, though."

"Didn't anyone ever tell you? The best things always come in small packages."

Chapter 7

Jarod stared at the two of them blankly, and Sandy gave a little cry of unease.

"I heard all about that guy. It was on the news. They said he escaped from some prison in Tennessee. That he's considered armed and dangerous."

"And he was staring into our bathroom window?" Jarod demanded.

They were all sitting in Dan's living room, near the fireplace and the beautiful floor-to-ceiling plate-glass windows. Reeves instantly went to pull the drapes; Sandy shivered, and Jarod continued to frown.

"I don't know if it was him or not, Jarod," Kelly tried to explain. "I saw something—"

"And I went outside," Dan told him patiently. "But whoever or whatever your mother saw was already gone. But if this guy *is* running around, it just seems safer if we stick together, huh?"

Jarod appeared to be a bit put out. "I can take care of her, you know," he told Dan indignantly.

Dan didn't take offense. He just smiled at Jarod easily. "I thought you might want to be near Sandy."

"Oh. Oh!" Jarod said.

"Should I make cocoa and more popcorn, Mr. Marquette?" Reeves asked smoothly.

"Sure, why not?" Dan replied. "Except that we'll have to take a quick run over to the McGraw house so Kelly and Jarod can get a few things for the night."

They all decided to go, except for Reeves, who intended to "repair the guest quarters" for the evening. Jarod started up again as soon as they were in the car, staring at his mother skeptically in the glow of the few streetlights they passed.

"I don't understand this. You saw these eyes. Dan went out, but nothing was there. And you didn't call the police for hours and hours? What were you doing in between?"

"Jarod!" Kelly exclaimed with exasperation. "I didn't know anything about this escaped convict until we got to dinner. We ran into June, and she told us about him. I hadn't seen the news. We called the police from the inn, and I assume they went out to look around."

Kelly twisted around in the seat. She saw that Jarod was staring at Sandy and that she was staring back at him—and that they seemed to be sharing a very knowing smile.

Well, she didn't owe those wayward teenagers any explanations, and she wasn't going to give them any.

Dan was gazing straight ahead, watching the road. "We don't know that it was the Peeper your mom saw, Jarod. It might just have been an animal."

Sandy shivered in the back. "From what they say, that man *is* an animal."

Jarod whispered something to her; Kelly heard a bit of it. Something about Sandy loving the animal in him. Sandy laughed, and Dan's knuckles whitened on the steering wheel.

"That's enough, you two!" he announced brusquely, and his voice was so stern that they both fell instantly silent. Kelly sank deeply into the seat and watched Dan, amused. Hmm. There was a double standard here. He might be a big boy and consider an affair of his choosing entirely proper—but though Sandy was pregnant and planning her wedding, Dan still wanted her to behave like a prim little girl.

Kelly shrugged and closed her eyes, still smiling. That was all right; she wasn't quite used to the situation yet, either. Sandy and Jarod were still kids, still dependent. She and Dan were neither.

They drove into her driveway. Jarod hopped out with Dan, determined to check the back of the house and study the tree and window area. Sandy and Kelly followed more slowly. Sandy was silhouetted by the streetlight, and Kelly found herself scrutinizing the girl anew.

She was so pretty. Tall, slim and very attractive. She had her father's coloring—including those dark eyes that could seduce like the devil's own. Her hair, too, was her father's. Longer, of course, falling down her back, but the same deep dark red, rich and luxurious.

There the similarities ended, because Sandy's features were delicate, unlike Dan's. Her face was a little heart, while his was an oval with a squared chin, broad cheekbones and a high forehead. Dan wasn't just tall, he was heavily muscular, and Sandy was far more fragile.

What was her mother like? Kelly wondered. And what woman could have walked away from the beautiful baby that Sandy must have been?

Sandy will never do that, Kelly thought, watching the girl. Somehow, she had grown up being very loving; the hurt that she must have endured hadn't made her bitter. Kelly bit her lower lip, thinking that Dan had done something very right with the girl. Oh, as people might say, Sandy had "gotten into trouble." But it was probably true that she had been doing what everyone else her age was doing—she and Jarod had simply been caught.

That didn't change the fact that she was a lovely girl. Quick to smile, polite, charming, eager to please. Dan had given her lots of love, enough for two parents, and it showed in everything about the girl.

She turned around suddenly, catching Kelly's intense scrutiny. "What's wrong?" she asked quickly.

Kelly grinned, shook her head and slipped her arm around Sandy's waist, then headed toward the house. "Nothing is wrong, Sandy, nothing at all. Come on, let's go in. You can help me get a few things."

It wasn't until they actually reached the house that Kelly remembered what an absolute mess everything was. Well, not everything, but her bedroom, certainly. They'd been running so late that the last thing in the world she'd been thinking of was the state of the bedroom. And if Jarod saw her bedroom . . .

If Sandy saw the bedroom . . .

"Sandy!"

"What?" Sandy asked, startled.

"Uh, run down to the basement for me, will you, please? There's a game tomorrow. Jarod's shoulder pads are down there, I think. Will you look for me, please?"

"Of course, Kelly, I'll be glad to."

Kelly stood there with a forced smiled plastered to her features until Sandy started toward the kitchen and the cellar stairs.

As soon as she was gone, Kelly spun around and raced up the stairs to her bedroom. The sheets weren't even attached to the bed anymore!

Desperately she made the bed, plumped the pillows and fixed the comforter. She was out of breath and gasping when she heard a voice behind her.

"Mom, why did you send Sandy down to the basement? My shoulder pads are in my locker."

"In your locker?" Kelly smiled and sat down on the bed. "In your locker. I didn't know."

"Kelly?"

Dan was suddenly at the door, staring at her anxiously. She saw that he, too, had remembered the state of her bedroom as soon as he entered the house.

She saw him stare a little incredulously at her fix-it job, relax and grin. "Uh, are we ready?"

"Just about."

"Okay. Sandy and I will be downstairs."

He disappeared, but Jarod stayed, staring suspiciously at Kelly. "Just what were you up to?"

"Just what are you talking about?"

"You two seem kind of chummy."

"Do we really?"

"Mom?" He moved into the room threateningly, all six-foot-two of him. "Mom, you're not ... ?"

"I'm not what?" she demanded indignantly.

To her chagrin, Jarod laughed and sat down beside her. Then he fell back to lie staring up at the ceiling in amazement, still laughing. "Oh, my! You two are on our cases, and you're up to the same thing!"

"Jarod! Who the hell told you I was up to anything?" Kelly was on her feet, staring at him coldly.

"Well, I don't see the difference—"

"I sure do, young man," Kelly said coolly. "I supported you; I raised you; I'm still trying to get you through college. In short, Jarod, you're still a kid, and you had no right getting that sweet young girl pregnant. Don't you ever question me, Jarod McGraw. I'm the parent and you're not. And it's just that simple!"

Furious, she turned her back on him and started out of the room, ignoring him.

"Mom!"

She heard him bolt from the bed; he caught up to her, placing his hands on her shoulders, whirling her around. She was about to snap at him, but she noticed that his eyes had the sheen of tears on them, that he wasn't being a wise guy anymore.

"I just want you to be careful," he whispered to her.

Her anger died. "Jarod . . ."

"Mom, face it, please, and don't get mad at me, but you're just a babe in the woods! He's been around. A lot. Sandy has told me that he's had, well, half a dozen affairs. She thinks that when her mother left he became very bitter. That he'll never trust a woman enough to really—to really fall in love again."

Kelly wondered at the truth of his words. She lowered her lashes, determined not to give anything away to him. "Jarod, Dan and I are just friends—a situation forced upon us by *your* situation. That's it. I'm fine. Okay?''

He nodded.

She smiled. ''You're making me forget everything! Go and get your stuff for tonight and tomorrow.''

He started walking down the hallway to his room. Kelly frowned, realizing that the light in his room was already on. Her heart suddenly started to flutter. She remembered that there was a lunatic loose in town. She didn't stop to think that her son was a foot taller than she was and over a hundred muscular pounds heavier.

At that moment she remembered only that he was her child, her baby. She went dashing after him and pushed by him, determined to meet the danger first, if the light signified danger.

It didn't. She dashed to his doorway, her heart pounding, to find Sandy sitting on his bed, serenely folding a pair of Jarod's underwear.

''Sandy!'' Kelly rasped out. ''What are you doing?''

''Packing for Jarod,'' Sandy replied.

Kelly suddenly thought that Dan wouldn't appreciate this sight at all. After all, it was one thing to know that his daughter was pregnant. It even seemed okay that he liked Jarod—after all, the two kids were going to get married. As of old, the situation was going to be honorably rectified. But this domesticity...

''Sandy! Go downstairs, please! Before your father comes up!''

Sandy rose gracefully and swept by Kelly, hurt and indignant. ''I've seen his underwear before,'' she murmured.

''Sandy!'' Jarod begged from behind Kelly.

Sandy disappeared. Kelly turned around to size up her son. He sized her up in return, and suddenly they both started to laugh.

He gave her a quick hug that threatened to break her ribs. She protested with a gasp, kissed his forehead and urged him to get going, promising that she would do the same.

A few minutes later they were ready to leave. Kelly locked everything up, wondering if spending a night away would do any good at all. They couldn't leave forever. If the police didn't get the Peeper tonight or tomorrow, she would have to come home anyway. The whole thing might be an exercise in futility.

But it was fun.

When they reached Dan's house, they found that Reeves had a massive pile of perfectly salted and buttered popcorn ready. He'd made hot chocolate, really good hot chocolate. And hers and Dan's, she discovered, had been spiked with just a touch of whiskey and crème de cacao.

They sat around in the living room watching an old World War Two movie on television, and Reeves—who had been in the RAF—told them what was real and what was pure invention.

She learned that Dan had met Reeves in West Germany where he had been stationed after a stint in Asia, and she worried just a little more about him. No one said it in so many words, but Kelly realized that Sandy's mother hadn't just walked out on him—he'd actually been in the service, overseas, when she had done it.

Maybe he never will trust a woman again, she thought, and then she tried to tell herself that she was making way too much out of everything. All they had

done was go to bed together, and as she had indicated
to Jarod, she was old enough to deserve some enjoyment in her life.

But it hadn't been just enjoyment. She knew that
she cared about him. That she hadn't been lying when
she'd said, "I think I'm in love."

That way of thinking could be very dangerous, Kelly
decided.

When the movie ended she offered to help Reeves
clean up. And when the cups and popcorn bowls had
been put away, she yawned and asked Sandy to show
her to her room. She said good-night to everyone,
avoiding Dan's eyes, and went up the beautiful, modern staircase.

Dan watched her go and wondered what she was
feeling, and why she had fled so quickly. He wasn't
tired himself; he felt restless, on edge, as if paradise
were still waiting for him.

The kids were still watching television, Dan murmured something and went into his office. He sat at
his desk in the dark, hiking his feet up on it and staring out into the night.

Insane. His behavior had been just about insane.
Dinner! So much for dinner, he scoffed. But a smile
curved his lips, and he didn't feel a bit guilty. He
wanted the whole house to go to sleep so he could
sneak around the darkened hallways like a kid and
find her.

Kelly...

He liked her name; he liked the rhythm of it. He
liked the smell of her perfume, and the way her hair
brushed against his shoulder or his hand.

He closed his eyes, leaning back. He'd had his share
of affairs; he'd never denied that. But he'd never tried

to pretend that something was more than what it was, and that was why he knew this was different.

It was more than wanting to touch her again—although he was just dying to do that! But he wanted to do more. He wanted to touch her and touch her and stay with her. Wanted to watch her eyes when they first opened with the day, as blue as the morning. Wanted to sleep with his hands tangled in that mass of blond hair. Wanted to watch her face when she bent over her work.

Wanted to protect her always from evil eyes that glowed in the dark, from anything hurtful in life. No one could do that, of course. But he wanted to be there with her to laugh at the good things, to hold her hand through the hard ones, to stand beside her through the bad times.

Dan started suddenly when he heard a tapping on his door. He frowned; Sandy never tapped; she just came in.

"Yes?"

Dan arched a brow as Jarod entered. He couldn't read the boy's expression in the darkness.

"Sir?"

"Jarod?"

"I, uh, well, I have to talk to you."

"Come on in. Turn on the light."

Jarod turned on the light, then looked awkward, as if he wished that he hadn't come. Dan pointed to the chair across from his desk. It was old and padded, with a dent in the seat. He'd had it forever; he took it with him every time he moved. It was Sandy's chair. From the time that she had been a little girl, she had perched in it, when she came to him with all her hurts and woes. She had never worried about coming to him when he was working; she knew she was welcome at any time.

She had sat in that chair to tell Dan tearfully that she was pregnant. It was probably the only time he hadn't really listened to her, Dan reflected. She had dropped her bombshell, and he had taken time only to learn the name of the boy—and then he had gone. To accost Kelly, to meet Jarod, and to realize that things could have been much, much worse.

Jarod sat in the chair, uncomfortably. Dan kept his feet stretched out on top of the desk, still relaxed, his slightly narrowed eyes the only sign that he was wary. What did Jarod know? How much had he sensed? "You wanted to speak to me?" he finally prompted.

"Yes."

Dan waited a minute. "Well?"

"Well." Jarod sat forward a bit. "Well, quite frankly, I'm worried about my mother."

"Oh."

"That's all?"

"Well, quite frankly, Jarod, I'm still worried about my daughter, so I suppose your concern is fair."

"You shouldn't be worried!" Jarod blurted out.

"Oh really?" Dan laughed. He was touched, but he was also irritated. After all, this was the kid who had gotten his daughter pregnant!

"Why, Jarod, shouldn't I be worried? You aren't exactly gainfully employed; you haven't got a home to offer her. You could go off and live in splendor and love and poverty, but I think that you're both too smart for that."

Jarod was quiet for a moment.

"I'm not trying to shove anything down your throat, Jarod," Dan added more kindly. "I want to help you both—so does your mother. You're both bright kids; you deserve a helping hand. Nor do we want to direct your lives; we just want to see that you get a fair shake. But don't tell me that I shouldn't be worried. Sandy is a baby about to have a baby. I still want to see her get an education. I want to see you get a good education, too, Jarod. You're tackling a massive responsibility. I'd be a fool if I weren't worried."

"Yes, that's true," Jarod replied softly. "But there's one thing you're forgetting. I love Sandy. I really love her. I'd give up anything—including my life—for her."

Something washed over Dan, something warm, something really beautiful. Jarod meant it. Maybe that was why Dan, as a father, had forgiven them both. Jarod *did* love Sandy—as much as she adored him. That total commitment they had to each other was rare, and very special.

"Yes, son. I believe that you do love her."

"And that's why I'm worried," Jarod returned. He was sitting very still, yet Dan knew that he was anxious, that coming in here had been one of the hardest things the boy had ever done.

"I guess that I want to know—just what are your intentions toward my mother?"

The words were ridiculously archaic, yet stated so seriously that Dan resisted the temptation to laugh. He thought about the question with his whole heart and mind and answered slowly. "I don't exactly know, Jarod. We don't know each other very well. I want to get to know her; I like what I know so far. I think that she's beautiful and charming."

"And...?"

"And I would never intentionally hurt her in any way. Does that satisfy you?"

Jarod stared at him levelly, then slowly smiled. "I think that you're falling in love with her!" he said smugly. Then he stood with sudden energy, stretching his hand across the desk, grasping Dan's and pumping it. "Yes, I am satisfied! Good night, sir!"

He left and the door closed sharply behind him.

Dan laced his fingers behind his head, smiling. "They're honorable, son," he said aloud softly. "My intentions toward your mother are quite, quite honorable."

And they were; he hadn't realized until just that moment how honorable they were, or exactly what his feelings had meant. He couldn't tell her yet, of course. She would think he was crazy.

He wanted to marry her. To have, to hold, from this day forth. To see those blue eyes open every morning, to sleep with his face against that blond hair. To be with her always.

He was in love. Jarod was one bright kid.

Kelly had thought she was exhausted, but once she got up to bed, all she did was toss and turn, then pause, staring up at the ceiling and smiling. She hugged her arms to her chest and remembered all the events of the day.

His eyes . . . she would never forget his eyes. Never forget the way he had looked at her when he had come up to the shower. How funny. They had said things to each other, yet she couldn't remember a word being spoken. All she could remember was the way he had looked at her.

And the way he had looked. So striking, so handsome, so masculine in that three-piece suit. And he had looked even better once the suit had been gone. As a matter of fact, she adored the way he looked. Every inch of him.

And how she missed him! She wished he was there, beside her now. The guest room had a wonderful queen-size bed, and the sheets smelled like fresh air and lemons. She would love to see him against them.

She frowned, reminding herself that the kids were in the house. That the kids—who had most obviously fooled around already, with obvious consequences—were not only in the house, but being kept chastely apart.

What an example I'm longing to set! Kelly thought dolefully. Then her frown deepened, because terrible or not, she wanted to be with him again. She wondered when—*if*—it would ever happen. It had been spontaneous the first time, but now she would worry and worry....

She should worry, she thought suddenly. She made a mental note to call her doctor right away. First thing Monday morning. She'd been yelling at Jarod about responsibility, but so far she had shown none herself. And neither had Dan. They hadn't been thinking. They had just looked at each other, then suddenly wound up in each other's arms, and then in her bed.

She started suddenly, hearing a noise in the hall. For a moment she panicked, thinking of the Peeper running around free. Then the fierce pounding of her heart subsided. This was Dan's house, and unlike her, he had a top-of-the-line security system. If you touched a window wrong in this place, an alarm would go off, summoning the police.

But someone was moving down the hallway. She could hear soft, furtive footsteps.

Hesitantly, Kelly reached for her robe and slipped into it, then crawled silently out of the bed. As quietly as she could, she tiptoed across the room to the door. She set her hand on the knob and twisted it slowly. She pulled the door open slightly and looked out.

There was someone moving down the hallway. Someone tall. Someone with gleaming blond hair.

Oh, Jarod, you little rat! Kelly thought. She slipped out into the hall, and a minute later he was almost on top of her.

"Ahem!" Kelly tapped her toe against the floor.

"Mom!"

"Jarod."

"I, uh, I thought I heard a noise."

She heard a furtive movement in the hall behind her and spun around expecting to find Sandy. "Dan!"

"Kelly, Jarod."

He was in a navy-blue bathrobe. Tall, mussed, and excessively alluring, Kelly thought, her heart hammering as she inhaled deeply, catching a whiff of his special scent. "Oh!"

There was another soft cry in the darkness. A feminine cry. Sandy.

"What in heaven's name—"

Light suddenly flooded the hallway. Reeves, gray hair untidy, face disgruntled, stared at them. "Begging your pardon, sir," he complained to Dan, "but just what is going on here?"

"I heard a noise in the hallway," Jarod explained quickly.

"That's funny," Dan said, eyeing him suspiciously. "I heard a noise out here, too."

Sandy laughed nervously. "Noises, noises."

"Yeah," Jarod murmured. "You know how old houses creak."

"This is a brand-new house," Dan reminded him.

"Oh. Well, new houses creak, too."

Suddenly Jarod didn't appear to be on the defensive anymore. He looked at Kelly, then at Dan, then back at Kelly, his eyes opening wide with alarm. "Mom! What are you doing out here?"

Kelly leaned back against her door and crossed her arms calmly over her chest. "Watching you try to sneak your way into Sandy's room."

"I suggest," Dan said, "that we all go back to bed."

"Oh my, yes!" Reeves interjected. "Yes, sir. I do recommend that you all go back to bed. To your separate beds. All of you."

Sandy didn't need any more prodding from anyone. "'Night, Dad. 'Night, Kelly... 'Night, Jarod."

She kissed her father, then Kelly. She never got a chance to kiss Jarod, because apparently Dan didn't even like the way she was *looking* at him.

"Good night, Sandra. Now!"

Sandy went fluttering away. Jarod smiled doubtfully. "Good night." But he didn't move.

Dan gave him a quizzical look.

"Fair is fair!" Jarod blurted suddenly turning to stare reproachfully at his mother.

"Oh, good heavens!" Kelly exclaimed.

She wasn't sure if she wanted to laugh, to slap her son for his insolence—or to cry. Because she didn't want to go to her bed alone.

But she did.

"Good night," she said to the three men, then stepped into her room and slammed the door.

Chapter 8

"Kelly, the doctor is ready to see you now."

Guiltily, Kelly set her magazine down and stood to follow the nurse into Dr. Barker's office. She'd had the most absurd notion after her examination—an intense longing to go running out of the office. She'd felt almost the same way over eighteen years ago when she had come to Dr. Barker and discovered that she was pregnant with Jarod. Small town living, she thought with a sigh.

She smiled at Joanie Simpson, Dr. Barker's nurse, and at Jill Hedrin, his office manager, then walked by them to take a seat in front of the doctor's enormous maple desk. Dr. Barker's glasses slipped down his nose a shade, and he pushed them back up. His hair was white, but his eyelashes were still pitch-black, and he had the bluest eyes that Kelly had ever seen. He folded his hands on his desk. "Kelly, you look just fine. As healthy as a horse."

"Thank you."

"If you don't hear from us, that means the results of the tests we took were fine, okay?"

"Great."

"And we'll take care of that birth control you were worried about, too."

She was thirty-five. She was probably the only woman in the world that age who had gone over six years without sex, she thought dryly. But here she was, blushing madly anyway.

"Congratulations, by the way."

"Pardon?"

"I'm the man who discovered that you were about to become a grandmother."

"Oh! Oh, well, I'm so glad. Not that I'm going to be a grandmother. I didn't mean that. I'm not miserable or anything—oh, brother! I'm glad that Sandy is coming to you. We've talked, of course. She's a lovely girl. She and Jarod—"

Dr. Barker interrupted her with a laugh. "Oh, I've heard all about things, though I'm probably the only one who has! They're a discreet couple. Your son told me he wasn't saying a word, just passing out a few wedding invitations when the time was right."

Kelly lowered her eyes and smiled. "Sandy is a sweet girl. I can't say I'm thrilled about the situation, but I'm very fond of her."

"And her father, I take it."

Kelly jerked her head up to stare at the doctor, but he was smiling at her innocently. "Small town!" she muttered dryly, and he laughed again and waved a hand in the air.

"I didn't say that, Kelly. I've just known you for a long time, young lady."

"I'm getting on for thirty-six, Dr. Barker!"

"And I'm closing in on seventy, so that makes you a young lady to me." He smiled. "Those two remind me so much of you and David. What a shame that you had to lose that man. I always liked him. Jarod is just like him—responsible, caring, loyal. I think he and Sandy are going to do just fine."

Kelly thanked him, then frowned suddenly. "Sandy is—she's fine, isn't she?"

"Fit as a fiddle. Nothing to be concerned about at all." He grinned. "That was her father's main worry, too. Nice man. I like him a lot. Yes, I like that man just fine."

Kelly grinned, she couldn't help it.

"Smart as a whip."

"Who?"

"That Dan Marquette. I've got some friends in Washington who've seen a lot of his work."

"Seen . . . ?"

"Programs at the museum to go along with his projects. Costume and military displays. I know people who have met him at cocktail parties and the like."

"I see." But she didn't. Dr. Barker was getting at something, but Kelly didn't know what.

Dr. Barker grinned at her. "You want to know what I'm getting at, don't you?"

Kelly laughed. "Well, yes, actually, I do."

"I just think you should take care, that's all. He's a man of experience, and you both need to remember that those two children are going to be depending on you. Be careful of how your own involvement affects their future."

"Humph!" Kelly said.

"What?"

"Humph! And I mean it. Dr. Barker." She leaned forward, planting her elbows on his desk. "No one gave me a hard time when I got pregnant with Jarod. I had a great father. But life was tough for us! We didn't get anything on a silver platter, and morés were different then, too. I had to let an awful lot slide off my shoulders. My God! Jarod and Sandy should be in seventh heaven! They're getting every bit of help imaginable. It isn't all worked out yet, but they'll both get to go to college. Sandy won't have to balance work with the baby just to send Jarod to school. He'll still get his scholarships, along with help from me. And as I'm sure you know, Mr. Marquette is in terrific financial shape."

"Don't resent him for it, Kelly."

"I don't."

"Maybe just a little?"

"Well, I'm not bitter, if that's what you're trying to say. A little envious, maybe. They're going to have it a hundred times easier than I did, that's all."

"They love each other, very much."

"I know," Kelly said softy. "And I'm glad."

"I never would have encouraged Sandy to marry Jarod if I hadn't believed that. Just like I wouldn't have encouraged you to marry David if I hadn't believed that you two loved each other." He sat back, his eyes twinkling. "I hear you're living with him."

Kelly gasped. "Well, you're wrong!" Her voice dropped, as if she were talking to herself. "I knew it was a mistake to go over there. In a small town..."

"Small town talk is thorough, Kelly. I've heard that you and Jarod have both been staying over there, and that the household is chaperoned by a very proper butler."

"Gentleman's gentleman," Kelly said.

"I beg your pardon?"

"Reeves calls himself a gentleman's gentleman," Kelly said, grinning. What relief! She felt vindicated. "And besides," Kelly said. "I'm not sure that you can actually live with a man who isn't in town."

"Flew back to D.C., did he?"

"You knew that, too?"

Dr. Barker lifted his hands. "Small town syndrome. When is he due back?"

"Today, tomorrow, I'm not sure."

"Well," the doctor mused, "I'm glad to see you smile, but I wouldn't have let anything bother you, anyway—people talking is nothing but a bunch of poppycock." He paused to wag a finger at her. "You just sit tight, Kelly McGraw. While that convict is running around, you opt for safety and don't you worry about anything anybody says, you hear me?"

Kelly smiled and nodded, then stood up to leave. "Dr. Barker?"

"Yes."

"Don't you worry about me. I have Jarod on my case as it is! I'm a big girl now, and even if I don't have Dan Marquette's experience, I do have . . ."

"What?"

"I'm not sure. Maybe it is not the quantity of experience—but the quality that counts. At any rate, I'm fine, and I can take care of myself."

"Good for you!"

Kelly left his office, smiled at his staff again and left. She felt like laughing, but also just a bit like crying. So, the whole town already knew what was going on. . . .

She was glad that she had come anyway. Actually, she'd had no choice. She was a responsible adult, and this time she was going to be prepared!

Prepared, and out of a job, she thought as she walked out to the parking lot.

She gnawed lightly on her lower lip. Dan and Jarod and Reeves had been insistent that she not go home alone, not with the Peeper on the loose. But she had work to finish. She could do preliminary drawings at Dan's, but she needed her board and her T-square and her pastels to do the final work.

Her work was a monthly project; *Dark of the Moon* was a comic book that came out twelve times a year, and she was lucky that she had just handed an issue in. But she was wasting an incredible amount of time. Dan didn't waste time, she reminded herself bitterly. He had needed to research something about the development of the flintlock pistol, so he had apologized profusely and taken off for Washington.

Kelly automatically headed for her own house. She just had to get some work done, or she would be up the creek without a paddle in a few days.

They would all be mad, of course. Men were like that. Jarod would be hurt that she hadn't asked him to come along, Dan would be furious, and Reeves would shake his head in that way that could make her want to crawl under a table.

"I can't stay away from my own house forever!" she said out loud. She paused in front of the house. Jarod would be at school for at least another hour. And Dan...

She hesitated, then decided not to park in the driveway. She went around to the old Ipsom house behind hers and parked underneath the oak. The Ipsoms wouldn't care; they had moved away almost five years ago, and the house was still up for sale.

Kelly was a little nervous when she let herself in, she hadn't been alone in the house since she had heard about the Peeper. But she locked the front door behind her and reminded herself that, after all, she hadn't been hurt, just frightened. The Peeper—if that's who the eyes had belonged to—hadn't been inside.

She would be fine. She'd just work for a few hours, lock up, then go back to Dan's, and no one would be the wiser.

And she felt good—really good! For the first time in years there was a man in her life. And what a man! She started humming and made herself a cup of coffee. Then she perched on her stool and stared down at her drawings. She picked up her pencil, and she was in such a good mood that she instantly had the White Knight rescue Daryl from a bubbling mire of black pitch, and Daryl was so taken by the kindness that he gave Esmeralda a clue to her lost brother's whereabouts.

Images seemed to fly onto the paper. But it was her hand that flew, she knew. There was just nothing like love.

"And I *am* in love!" she whispered.

Only then did her hand pause. Was she really in love? Could love come that quickly? She wouldn't dare to tell Dan that she loved him. It was one thing to murmur in the afterglow of passion—weren't men famous for doing just that?—but quite another to come right out and say it calmly and in all seriousness.

She sighed softly. Jarod seemed to be determined to warn her against the man who was going to be his fa-

ther-in-law. Even Dr. Barker seemed ready to warn her
about Dan.

"But I believe in him!," she told her pictures. "And
I believe in me. It's just that..."

Her voice trailed away. It was just so soon. There
was being in love, and there was being in love with
being in love, and she had been alone for a long, long
time. She knew that at first she had been in love with
being in love with David, the real emotion had grown
slowly. Time and experience, the good and the bad,
had made their love stronger and deeper, year by year.

But falling in love was the first step. The emotion
couldn't grow if you didn't allow it to. If you didn't
take chances.

Suddenly she knew that she was willing to take
chances. All kinds of chances. Even if it meant getting hurt. This would be a different kind of relationship. An adult relationship. There wouldn't be any
"have tos" this time. She wouldn't have to marry him.
If and when things went further, she would know this
time that it was exactly what they both wanted. Smiling, Kelly took a sip of her coffee. And then she froze.

Someone was at her front door.

She slid off her stool, determined to walk calmly out
to the hallway and look through the little peephole. It
was probably the mailman, she told herself as she
paused in the doorway. Or maybe...

It wasn't the mailman, and it wasn't anyone else legitimate. People who came to your door generally rang
the bell or used the knocker—and her front door was
already opening.

Kelly panicked, then told herself that she couldn't
panic. She had to hide, and she had to find something
with which to defend herself.

She looked around desperately. Oh, God! Why did she have to be an artist? A pencil wasn't exactly the best weapon in the world!

Glancing quickly around the room, she saw a heavy vase sitting over by the window. She grabbed it, then looked for someplace to hide. An artist's drawing table didn't provide the greatest cover in the world, either—a nearsighted slug would see her under it!

Menacing. As if someone knew that she was in the house. As if someone knew...and was stalking her.

"Oh, God!"

The words were a silent whisper on her lips. She looked at the phone, but it seemed so far away. And even if she did reach it, the intruder would hear her.

And the footsteps were coming closer. Any minute now the intruder would be in the room with her.

Kelly made a mad dive for the doorway, then stood there, praying that the ragged sound of her breathing wasn't really as loud as it sounded to her. This couldn't be happening, she told herself.

But it could.

The footsteps were coming closer. And closer.

She would have very little chance, she knew. She would have to strike immediately, strike hard, strike for all she was worth, and then run like the wind. Strike and run, strike and run....

The footsteps hesitated just outside the doorway, as if the intruder knew that she was there, just feet away. Waiting.

Another step.

He was there; one more step and she would have to strike. She couldn't freeze, because if she did, it would be all over.

A floorboard gave; the step was taken.

Kelly let out a loud, desperate cry, then rushed from her hiding place behind the door with the vase raised. The intruder's head, she noticed in an instant, was way above her. The room was dim and shadowy—crash!

And—slam!

She was gripped violently by the shoulders, then slammed back hard against the wall, a prisoner in his arms....

"Kelly!"

She heard her name as she was released, and she realized dimly that it had been shouted out just after her vase had come down on the man's head, just as she had come very close to hysteria, aware that she had been caught, and that her captor was far more powerful than she was.

"Oh!" she cried. Her panic faded instantly as she stared with dismay at Dan.

Dan, who was holding his head between his palms and staring at her in return.

"Dan! What are you doing here?"

"What the hell are *you* doing here?" he demanded furiously in return.

"I live here!"

"But you're not supposed to be here!"

"Neither are you!"

"Ooh...damn!" he groaned, and felt his head gingerly. He turned back into the hall, then headed for the kitchen. Nervously, Kelly followed him. He was digging into the freezer for ice. She ran to a drawer to dig out a towel to hold the ice for him. Still staring at her furiously, he slid into a chair at the kitchen table.

"Here, let me help you," she offered.

"No! Leave me alone!" He snatched the ice from her and held it up to his temple. "Damn," he muttered again.

She slid into a chair opposite him, her remorse disappearing in a rush of resentment. Men! It was almost as if they wanted you to be helpless, because as soon as you did something to fend for yourself, they were ready to kill you.

"Don't keep looking at me like that! This is my house. You were the one sneaking around in it."

"I wasn't sneaking around. And you're not supposed to be here! Damn you, Kelly, there's a lunatic on the loose—"

"I have to work for a living. You know that."

"I know that you're as defenseless as a two-pound puppy!"

"Then why are you holding ice on your head?"

He let out a loud oath, dropped his ice and suddenly gripped Kelly, dragging her onto his lap, where he held her tightly in his arms.

"Let me go!"

He did, and she slid onto the floor. In fury she quickly scrambled to her feet and left the kitchen. So much for love! She couldn't be in love with this stupid macho masher!

"Kelly!"

He was right behind her, catching her shoulders. She tried to shake him off, but you just didn't shake off a man like Dan Marquette. Before she knew it she was backed against the wall again, staring into those deadly dark and ridiculously sexy eyes of his. And despite the fact that she was furious, she was achingly aware of his body, hard and strong and very male, against hers, pinning her there. She was aware of his hands on her shoulders, of the feel of his fingertips.

She could feel his arms, and she could feel his hips, and she was sure that he was every bit as aware of her as she was of him. He, too, felt that incredible rush of instant desire, and that desire was growing, hot and hard against her, even as they stood there, ready to do battle.

"Fool!" he said suddenly, softly, harshly... heatedly.

"Fool!" Kelly repeated.

"I'm sorry!" he said, and his hands were on her cheeks then, and he was staring down into her eyes, staring with the same hunger that she felt. "Kelly, I was scared to death for you, that's why I yelled. That's why—"

"What are you doing here?" she asked a little desperately. "You're not supposed to be in town. How did you get in?"

He was leaning closer to her. Once again, words didn't matter.

"I have Jarod's key. They're coming to put in a security system, and I had to be here. And I didn't tell you because I was pretty sure that you wouldn't have let me do it."

"I wouldn't have . . . I won't," she protested, but it didn't matter. His mouth came down on top of hers. Possessed it, owned it, ravaged it—and it was wonderful.

"Oh..."

They broke apart to breathe, and she slipped her arms around his neck, then pressed her face to his shoulder. His hand went to her throat and then her breast, and she thought of all the times when she had

wanted so desperately to be with him, when they
hadn't touched each other, hadn't dared, because
Sandy and Jarod were with them.

"Kelly..."

"Dan..." she whispered in return. She wasn't mad
anymore; she was elated. Thrilled that they had both
chosen to come here, because finally, finally, they were
alone again.

"I've missed you, I've missed your scent, and I've
missed the feel of you. I've never known anything
softer..."

"Oh, Dan..."

"Or more beautiful. There's nothing more like spun
gold than your hair, and—"

"Dan!"

"Kelly, darling..."

"No, no, Dan, listen! There's someone at the door
again! Someone just standing there!"

He swallowed sharply, then gave himself a shake
and drew a ragged breath. "Oh, Lord."

"Dan, listen!"

He broke away from her, bringing a finger to his
lips. He walked silently over to the door, then gazed
through the peephole. Kelly watched him step back, a
look of incredulous dismay on his face.

Then he threw the door open.

Jarod was standing there, smiling, a little confused.

"Dan, my mother's car is out back. I thought you
weren't going to tell her. I thought that this was going
to be a surprise."

"Oh, yeah. It's been a great surprise."

"She knows?"

"Hmm. She knows."

Jarod stepped into the house, then whistled softly. "What happened to your head? It's bleeding."

"It's just a scratch. I ran into a vase."

"Ran into a vase?" Jarod murmured, frowning, but then he paused, turning around at the sound of slamming car doors coming from the driveway. "Oh, they're here! The security guys."

Dan nodded. "Let them in, will you, Jarod? I've already talked to them; they know what to do."

He turned to walk back into the kitchen. Jarod started, suddenly noticing Kelly, who smiled uneasily and raced after Dan.

He had slumped back into a chair at the kitchen table and picked up the towel to wipe the little trickle of blood off his forehead.

"Dan," Kelly said hesitantly. Then, more surely, she repeated, "Dan, I can't let you do this. I don't know what a good security system costs, but I can't afford it right now, and I can't let you—"

She broke off, because his expression had become dark and furious. "Dan?"

He stood up slowly. "Kelly, I can't take it anymore. Can you? Hell, I didn't have to leave town! I just couldn't bear your being in a bed in my house without me in that bed, too!"

"But... but..."

"Kelly, you can let me put this system in so that you and Jarod can come home, or we can say the hell with whatever the kids are going to think and you can move into my bedroom. I can't stand this any longer. This is the most ridiculous relationship in the world! We're adults, but we're trying to act chaste because that's the way we want our kids to behave. But it's too late. And I'll be damned if I'm going to do it any longer!"

Kelly inhaled slowly and shakily. He was making her furious, and she didn't like his set of choices!

"Mom!" Jarod called from the living room. "They need to talk to you out here!"

She stared back at Dan and swallowed hard. She was in love with him, and, so help her, was beginning to think that he loved her, too. But she didn't quite have the nerve yet to accept her son's condemnation, to set that love before the world.

"You'll be able to come home Friday or Saturday," Dan said harshly.

"Mom!"

She felt all the tension—sexual, wonderful, frightening, taut and furious—in the man before her.

"I—I'm coming," Kelly called to Jarod.

She was a coward. She wanted to love him, and she wanted to give herself to him completely. But not yet. Not quite yet.

She hurried out to the living room, feeling his eyes boring into her back.

Chapter 9

On Saturday afternoon they all went to Jarod's game; it was an all-star game, with the income from ticket sales going to a local charity.

Jarod, Kelly noted, shone. He outdid even himself that day. He couldn't miss. If he passed, the ball was caught. If he ran, he gained yard after yard.

Sitting in the stands, watching her son, Kelly felt set apart, alone despite the roar of the crowd. She felt as if she had managed to escape from her body, from her self, and stare down at Jarod, the past, the present—and the future.

Don't take it too much to heart, she warned him silently. Don't fall in love with the adulation of the crowd.

She knew how the afternoon would go, and she was a little worried. When the game was over, every girl from ten counties was going to cast herself at that perfect blond giant. And Jarod was only human, and capable of being a hell of a flirt.

Kelly came out of her reverie when she heard someone shout, "Kill 'em, McGraw! Kill 'em out there!"

Nice sentiment for teenagers, she decided wryly, but, hey, she thought sarcastically, why not get them set for real life?

They managed to fall in love in the midst of all this, Kelly reminded herself. Jarod and Sandy had fallen in love despite everything going on around them. Sandy was probably the most beautiful girl in the class—or in ten counties. They would be okay, Jarod and Sandy. They'd chosen each other, and no matter what, they would stay in love. It was foolish to worry.

"He's great. He's not just good, he really has the seeds of greatness," Dan said softly, next to her.

He sounded surprised. Kelly thought she probably should have resented that, but she shrugged, thinking that it was too beautiful a day for her to resent anything. She said only, "He plans to play through college."

"He could probably go pro," Dan said.

I don't want him to go pro, Kelly thought, but she didn't say it out loud. She'd never even said it out loud to Jarod; it wasn't her decision.

He wanted to go into law and politics. Jarod could get as excited about an intriguing court case as he could a football, and Kelly personally thought that a life spent in the pursuit of learning had to be better than a life spent having one's knees put back together.

She shrugged. "He knows his capabilities and his options. He'll have to decide when the time is right."

Dan laughed softly, catching her hand, lacing his fingers through hers. "So if luck goes your way, he won't play pro ball, huh?"

"Dan, that's not—"

His laughter, warm and husky, caught her up, and she glanced quickly into his eyes to discover that he wasn't taunting her—he simply understood. Understood that she would never want to sway Jarod—and also that she did hope he wouldn't go pro.

"Oh, go buy some peanuts, will you!" she snapped.

"Peanuts aren't going to solve our problems, Kelly."

"I don't know what you're talking about."

"You know exactly what I'm talking about."

"I—"

"Tonight, Kelly."

"Dan—"

"I'm not going to sneak into your room in the middle of the night. You'll be back home, and I'll be damned if this is going to go on any longer. Tonight we'll go out—"

"Dan, I can't talk about this in the middle of the game!"

"You have to talk about it in the middle of the game. Because later the kids will be back, and I know you—you won't want to talk in front of them."

"Dan!"

She swung around to face him. Her eyes were so crystalline and beautiful that he thought he would go insane. He could just see the headlines: Scholar Attacks Mother of All-Star Hero in Stands—Plot Thickens: Scholar's Daughter Pregnant by Hero!

"Dan!" she whispered suddenly, vehemently. "You know I want to be with you!"

"You will be." He paused and looked at her intently.

"Kelly, we're the adults! If they don't like something, that's their problem."

"Dan, please, go buy some more peanuts."

"Okay, but we'll still have to settle this later."

He left her in the stands and went to buy a sack of the hot roasted nuts. Kelly smiled, watching him. She had noticed that a lot of the fans in the stands were also watching him. She didn't mind. It was actually rather nice. He seemed to draw everyone's eyes—but he was hers.

Pride, Kelly, she warned herself, goeth before a fall.

Someone hailed him when he started back up the stadium steps. It was Sandy, Kelly saw. She was sitting with a group of her girlfriends about ten tiers below them.

Dan saw his daughter and waved, and Kelly noticed that all the girls were giggling and blushing, looking up at him from under their lashes. Little twits! Kelly thought. But then she leaned back, grinning. Sandy was tangling a dark lock of hair around her finger as she spoke to her father, and she looked proud. Wonderfully proud. All your friends think your father is a doll, and that's great, Sandy! Kelly thought. More power to you.

The girl might need that today. She looked a little tense. She was smiling, but she was tense.

Because a lot of girls were watching Jarod, too, watching him like tigresses on the hunt.

He won't hurt you, Sandy! Kelly wanted to promise her. He'll smile, because he's Jarod. He'll be flattered, and he'll be polite. But he really loves you, and he would never hurt you. I hope you know that!

"Peanuts?"

"What?" She started. Dan was back, peanuts in hand.

She dug into the bag for one, and popped it into her mouth. She turned curiously, aware that Dan was watching her.

"Umm," he said.

"Umm?"

"I just love the way you did that." He gripped her hand and kissed her fingertips. "Salt. Umm."

His eyes, his touch . . . arousal soared through her. She snatched her hand back, certain that she was as crimson as a freshly boiled lobster, and that anyone who glanced her way would know exactly what she was thinking.

"Would you stop that!"

"Stop what?"

"Dan Marquette . . ."

"Shh! Watch your son. This is it! Thirteen seconds remaining, eleven, ten—"

The clock ticked down, and the game was over. The rest of the players on the winning team plucked Jarod up off the ground and lifted him up like a god, while the crowd screamed and people began to rise from the stands.

Kelly stood hastily, feeling uneasy, although she wasn't sure why. Then she saw Sandy's face, just for a minute, and it was sad. Pathetic, really. She looked so strained and worried and unhappy. . . .

If only I could reach her! Kelly thought trying without thinking to move forward. But there was a giant surge going on. The only thing that kept her from falling was the fact that Dan slipped his arms around her waist and held her close to his chest while the wave of people rushed past.

"Hey!" he warned her. "What do you think you're doing?"

"What? Oh!" He grabbed her hand and started to lead her downward. "Dan, I was going to try to see Sandy."

He paused, arching one brow. "Not your son? Hey, you're the mom of the hour, Mrs. McGraw. Don't you want to go revel for a minute in maternal pride?"

He was teasing her—nicely.

She shook her head.

"Oh, I see," he said, making it obvious that he didn't see at all. "You're not proud of your son?"

"Of course I am!" Kelly protested. "It's just that he certainly doesn't need me right now. I'd rather see Sandy for a minute."

Dan's eyes narrowed slightly, and he stood still, forcing her to face him and do the same. She tossed her hair back and planted her hands on her hips, but she didn't speak.

"You're worried about Sandy?"

She didn't know if it was a question or an accusation.

"No, I'm not worried about Sandy."

"Yes, you are. Why?"

"I'm not! I wanted to see her, that's all!"

A short, fat, balding man in a hurry suddenly slammed against Kelly, and she stumbled against Dan. He stopped scowling long enough to catch her and hold her while the bald man apologized.

And while he was still holding her, June chose to come by. Tall, slinky, sexy—interested—June. "Hi, you two! Don't you look cozy.'' She smiled secretively as she met Kelly's eyes.

Kelly felt embarrassed and looked away, yet when Dan released her, she wasn't sure that she wanted to be released.

"Hello, June, how are you?" he asked.

"Fine, fine. Oh, Kelly! Aren't you proud of that son you've got? He's just fabulous!" June winked at Dan. "That pretty little girl of yours is going to have to watch out, isn't she?"

"Sandy?" Dan smiled. "Sandy will be fine; she can take care of herself."

"Well, I was just so surprised," June said, looking curiously at Kelly. "I ran into Ted Pinder—he's my nephew," she explained quickly for Dan's benefit. "And he's in Jarod's class at school. Those kids haven't told anyone about their wedding! They haven't whispered a word of it to a single soul."

Kelly glanced quickly, uncomfortably, at Dan, but he was looking pleasantly at June.

He shrugged. "Well, a wedding is a big thing in life, June. Maybe, at the moment, they like keeping it as their secret. You know how kids are."

"And how love is," Kelly added sweetly, careful not to look at Dan. "It's so special sometimes that you don't even want to tell the one you're in love with!"

June chuckled softly. And then someone plowed into Kelly again, sending her flying against Dan once more. This time it was Sandy who had bumped into her. Sandy, smiling away with a fresh young beauty to rival the sun, apologizing and asking if she and Jarod could do something that night, all in one breath.

"Hold it! Hold it!" Dan commanded, and he forced her to calm down long enough for a quick introduction to June.

Sandy replied courteously, then started pleading once again. "Everyone is going, Dad! I mean everyone—"

"Jarod isn't," Kelly interrupted dryly. "Because he hasn't said a word to me yet."

"Oh!" Sandy spun around. "Oh, Kelly, he will! He's just having a hard time getting away from the other kids." She paused. Her words had held a touch of bitterness. Then her enthusiasm for her current project washed away the ill feelings. "Dad, Kelly, really, it's totally innocent, and it sounds wonderful!"

"Totally innocent?" Laughing, Dan looked at Kelly. She lowered her lashes, trying to indicate June's presence.

"Totally innocent," he repeated, grinning down at his beautiful daughter. "What are you talking about, Sandra?"

"Oh! The coach—" She swung around again to face Kelly earnestly. "Coach Harrison. Jarod says you've known him for years and years, and that you respect him and trust him and think that he's wonderful—"

"Wonderful?" Dan interrupted, looking at Kelly.

"He was my swimming coach when I was in high school."

"He's at least sixty, if he's a day," June volunteered with a chuckle, smiling at Dan.

"Go on, Sandy," Kelly urged.

"Well, Coach Harrison said he wants to take the team up to Skyline Drive for the night. There's a spe-

cial nature hike first thing in the morning. Coach said
that he'd take the first string and—"

"Since when are you first string?" Dan demanded.

Sandy stopped, blushing. "Da-aad!" she wailed.
"It's not just Coach Harrison going! It's his wife, and
two other teachers and their wives, and six other girls.
Honest, Dad. Separate cabins—and Mrs. Harrison
will be in with us."

Dan glanced over at Kelly. She smiled, knowing that
he was trusting to her greater knowledge of the situation. Whatever you decide, he was telling her, and she
was glad of his trust.

Dan lowered his eyes quickly. Kelly! Let them go! he
pleaded silently, hoping she would read his thoughts.
Please, decide to let them go. We'd finally have a
chance!

But he couldn't say it. He had to let her decide. He
couldn't, as a responsible parent, make that kind of a
decision just because he was so frustrated that he
might self-destruct in a matter of minutes. Nor, if the
decision were made the way he hoped, did he want to
be the one to make the first move. He had to be sure
that she wanted him as much as he wanted her.

"I think it'll be okay," Kelly said slowly. She was
barely able to finish speaking before Sandy threw her
arms around her and nearly suffocated her with grat-
itude. "Oh, Kelly! Thank you, thank you! I'll go tell
Jarod. Oh, thank you! Thank you!"

She went rushing away. Kelly and Dan stared at each
other, laughed, then shrugged.

"Well, how nice for both of you!" June exclaimed.

"Pardon?" Kelly asked.

"Well, you've just sent the kids off until tomorrow." June's voice lowered insinuatingly. "You've got the entire night to yourselves."

For a moment Kelly wanted to smack the other woman, but then she noted the amusement with which Dan was watching her, and she burst out laughing.

"Oh, June! You're right!" Try to get me in trouble, will you? she thought silently. She decided to play up to June's expectations.

"Dan, what should we do?" she asked sweetly.

This time he slipped his arms around her just for the pure enjoyment of it, drawing her back against his chest and resting his chin thoughtfully on top of her head. Steady! he warned himself. Steady...

He answered her thoughtfully.

"Hmm. I say dinner on the highway. That new place that just opened. I hear it's wonderfully romantic. Italian food, great wine, and a strolling violin player. Then we can catch the last ghost tour, and then..." He winked at June and lowered his lips to Kelly's ear and whispered "What am I supposed to do here? Should I say that I'll get you chastely home by eleven? Or should I let her tell the town that a deliciously illicit affair is going on?"

Kelly lowered her head quickly to keep from laughing. "Oh, Dan!" she exclaimed. "Oh, Dan..."

"Whoa," June muttered, gazing at them both. "I guess I'll step out of this one. It's getting uncomfortably hot for a girl without a date for this evening. Excuse me, and do have fun! After all, that's what you're planning to do, isn't it?"

Kelly twisted around to stare up at Dan mischievously. Neither of them even noticed when June smiled, waved and left them.

"That was really good, Kelly," Dan said in awe. "That friend of yours will have our names bandied all over town, you know. You've already taken a nose dive from propriety, Mrs. McGraw."

"Have I?" Kelly demanded innocently.

"Yes," he told her somberly. "But then, since you have . . . well, we can't let you have this horrible reputation—not unless you've really earned it."

"I'm just dying to earn it!" Kelly retorted. She moved closer to him in her excitement, taking both his hands, holding them between hers.

"Dan, I own a cabin up in the mountains. It's the most beautiful place in the world. There's a stream and a fireplace, and deer that eat right out of your hand. You've never seen anyplace so peaceful. The tour ends at ten—"

"Who needs the tour?" Dan choked out.

"You do!" Kelly laughed. "Honest, it's great. I can't believe you've missed it this far. But after—"

"You've got a date, Mrs. McGraw. Shall we collect our offspring and hurry them on their way?"

"Sounds good to me!"

Kelly was grateful that Jarod was still so keyed up from his game—and so grateful to have been given permission to take off overnight—that he didn't spend much time harassing her.

He spent the drive home chatting away in amazement. He hadn't been that hot, he assured her, it was just that the other team's defense was clumsy. "It all just went my way, Mom. Like those guys had butterfingers."

When they reached the driveway she smoothed over the first touch of trouble easily. Jarod, frowning as he reached into the trunk to bring out his gear, stopped cold to look at Kelly.

"Mom, they haven't caught this Peeper guy, have they?"

"Not that I know of."

His shoulders seemed to sag, as if the weight of the world had settled over them. "I can't—I mean, this overnight thing, it isn't that big a deal."

Kelly inhaled sharply. "What are you talking about?"

"You! Oh, Mom! I can't leave you here! Not when the guy might have been staring right at you."

"There's a brand-new security system in this house!"

"But you would be alone! You shouldn't be alone. I don't care how good that security system is."

"Really, Jarod, it isn't necessary for you—"

"Mother," Jarod replied primly, "you must know that for a parent you are...very nice-looking." He grinned a little crookedly. "I've actually gotten into a few fights 'cause of you, you know. That sickie would think he'd died and gone to heaven if he found you alone."

Kelly listened to his words in amazement, blinked, and nodded slowly. "Thank you for the compliment—I think. But, Jarod, I won't stay here. I'm going to the new Italian restaurant with Dan and—"

"Oh! You can go back over there for tonight! And I won't have to worry, because Reeves will be there!"

"I could, uh, stay with Dan, yes."

He smiled, relieved. He actually patted her on the back, then started for the house.

Kelly waited behind him guiltily for a moment. He was whistling, by then. She shrugged and followed him. She hadn't lied to him; he had simply made some assumptions. He was anxious to see things his way because he wanted to go on his little trip; why should she correct him?

By the time she reached the front door, he was upstairs in the shower. By the time she had her sneakers untied, he was out, clad in his briefs, drying his hair briskly with a towel.

"Can I take the car?

Kelly lifted her shoulders and frowned curiously. "Doesn't Sandy have her own car? A nice one."

"Yeah. Yeah. It's nice. I just like..." He hesitated. "I just like to drive my own car now and then. Well, your car." He cast her a pleading look. "I really need a car, Mom. One of my own."

"You're going to need lots of things," Kelly said softly.

He winced, and she was suddenly sorry. Today had been such a high for him; he deserved to spend the rest of it being young. Young and totally carefree.

But it's true! she thought. They're rich, and we're not. I can't just run out and buy you a sports car, Jarod. I'm worried about helping you to simply survive. If your wife-to-be has a car, you're going to have to swallow your pride and learn to love it!

"You're welcome to the car," she said lightly, tossing her sneakers into her closet. "It even has a full tank of gas."

He nodded, and thanked her for the keys she handed him. "I'm going to get dressed. When is Dan supposed to be here?" he asked.

"Soon, I guess."

"I'll stay until he gets here."

"You don't have—"

"I do. Go on, take your shower. I'll be downstairs. And if you see anything, scream your head off. I may not be old, but I promise, I'm tough."

Kelly laughed, brushing his cheek with her knuckles. "I know you're tough, hotshot. And, hey, I was proud of you today," she added softly.

He grinned. "I know, Mom. Thanks." He gave her a quick hug, then turned back to his own room.

A little nervously, Kelly threw off her dirty clothes and stepped beneath the shower. She was glad that Jarod had decided to wait with her. She didn't touch the curtain; she couldn't even bring herself to glance at the window.

Maybe it had just been a raccoon, she said, trying to reassure herself. But she knew that it would be a long, long time before she would ever feel comfortable in this shower again.

Alone.

With that thought she started smiling, because she had been just fine when Dan had been in there with her.

And they would have all night tonight. All night. Up at the cabin. Her cabin...

She paused, remembering Jarod's admission that they had used her cabin when Sandy had gotten pregnant. And, of course, Jarod had come into existence in that cabin.

But it still meant everything good to her. Everything good in the world. Stillness, peace, beauty. The sound of the creek, the magic of the sky, the fearless ease of the deer and squirrels. The cabin had been David's, and it represented everything good about David, too.

"I loved you," she whispered aloud. "I really loved you, David McGraw."

But he was gone, and he'd been gone a long time. They had lived together long enough to know that love wasn't just a fantasy, that it was real. Could be real again.

And then she realized that she was standing in the shower, not moving. She turned off the faucet and gave her head a little shake. Strangely, everything felt very good. David wouldn't begrudge any of them the cabin. He would secretly have laughed if he'd known about Jarod and Sandy....

Just as he had always smiled when the cabin and Jarod's name had been mentioned together.

He would smile now. He could be jealous, he could be possessive—he could be a lot like his son. But he would like Dan Marquette. Kelly felt it with certainty, and that made her feel very, very good about herself. And about the evening ahead.

Jarod let Dan in when he came to the front door. They talked about the game for a moment, and Jarod asked Dan if he wanted anything to drink, and Dan said no.

Then, to Dan's surprise—he'd been as careful as possible about the things he had said—Jarod let out a great sigh of relief. "I'm so glad my mother is spending the night with you!"

"Ah—what?" Dan asked, sure that he must have heard wrong.

"With this Peeper guy running around."

"Oh, yes."

Jarod grinned. "Old Reeves can hear a pin drop, you know. I leaned over to give Sandy a kiss on the cheek when we were watching TV, and the next thing I knew, he was standing between us.''

Dan looked over at Jarod and nodded. He was grateful when Jarod kept talking.

"Thanks for letting us go on this trip. It's going to be great. We're going to have a wonderful time. Apart—I mean. That is, we'll be together, but—''

Dan swallowed and waved a hand nonchalantly. "I know what you're saying, Jarod.''

"Yeah. Well, if you're here, I'm going to go, then. Is Sandy ready?''

"I'm sure she is. Reeves was packing for her.''

"Wish I had Reeves,'' Jarod murmured, then looked at Dan guiltily. "I didn't mean that she was spoiled, or anything.''

"She probably is—in some ways,'' Dan said.

Jarod nodded. "Okay. I'm going. Have a good time. Well, don't have *too* good a time.''

"Good bye, Jarod. And be careful.''

"We will be.''

Jarod waved to Dan. Dan heard him run up the stairs to say goodbye to his mother, then rush back down and out the front door.

Kelly came downstairs a few minutes later. Dan could just see her through the doorway, and he stood, a bit awed despite the fact that he felt he was getting to know her pretty well.

She looked . . . beautiful. She was wearing an emerald-green knit dress with a mandarin collar and long sleeves, and the hemline fell well below her knees. Despite that, it was one of the most sensual garments he'd ever seen. It fell over her breasts like a whisper, swirled around her hips, and made her waist something that he'd die to touch, to slip his hands around....

He didn't realize that he was staring until she smiled a bit nervously and hurried to him, clasping his arms and rising up on tiptoe to kiss him, then twirling around in front of him and glancing back at him anxiously.

"Well?"

He laughed ruefully. "Lust is roaring through me," he told her honestly. *More than lust, Kelly,* he added silently. *Much, much more!*

She turned pink and smiled, and his body caught on fire. So much of what he saw consisted of lies, games, pretenses—but not Kelly. She was so honest. Honest about wanting him, honest about hesitating. So willing to give, but just a little bit shy about giving.

He laughed again, reached for her hand, pulled her back to him and kissed her. She smelled like heaven. He didn't know if it was a scented soap or an exotic and subtle perfume, but it was a temptation he knew he wouldn't be able to resist. Drawing a ragged breath, he set his hands on her shoulders and smiled ruefully.

"We'd better get going. I made reservations."

She nodded, then said, "Oh! Wait!"

He frowned and waited in the hallway while she raced back up the stairs, and when she came back down toting a massive suitcase he stared at her, puzzled.

"For one night?"

"Ah, but you don't know what's in it."

"A hot tub?"

"Ha ha."

He took the suitcase from her and marvelled at its weight. She was small, but strong and tough. "Hot bricks?" he asked.

"Never you mind, Mr. Marquette."

He took her keys and locked the door as they left the house, telling her about Jarod's comments while they walked to his car.

Kelly shrugged, unhappy, but philosophical. "They'd just never understand the difference," she murmured.

"Is there really such a difference?" Dan asked her ruefully, once they were in the car and out on the road. "Kelly, think about it. They're expecting a baby, and we all know how Sandy got that way! In another few months they'll be married, living together. And we're behaving as if they shouldn't kiss!"

Kelly looked down at her hands. "Dan, we can't condone anything else!"

"I know."

They rode in silence for a few minutes. He glanced her way several times and saw that she was still watching her hands, so he kept his silence.

When they reached the restaurant he ordered champagne, and when he made a toast, it was to her dazzling, open, honest, beautiful blue eyes. She laughed, but then he made another toast, very seriously, to another kind of beauty.

He took her hand across the table. "Kelly, thank you. Thank you very much...for tonight. For inviting me someplace that is really special to you."

She moved her fingers idly over his hand, tracing the pattern of the veins. She looked back up at him at last, and he knew that he was staring at her intently, too intently. But he loved her so much that he wanted to learn everything there was to know about her, yet at the same time he knew that the search might take him a lifetime.

"Hey!" she protested. "People are looking at us." She smiled playfully trying to break the mood. "I think it's because I'm so short and you're so tall."

"I think it's because you're beautiful."

She grinned again, still playing wistfully with his hand. "I think it's because *we're* beautiful—together. Dan, thank you. I feel beautiful with you. Young and beautiful."

He sipped his champagne, leaning back to study her with wry amusement. "You are young."

"Not that young. Just short."

"You're not that short. Five-three is respectable.

"Wonderful. I'm only five-two. Against six-four."

He shrugged. "Six-three. See?"

She nodded sagely. "I'm still short."

"Young and beautiful. Come on, Kelly, tell me. Just how young?"

"Well, I'm not underage."

"Thirty-four to thirty-six?"

She twirled her champagne glass, watching the liquid and not him. "Thirty-six in October."

He whistled softly. "Aha!"

"Aha, what?" She stared at him, then flushed. "Well, it was never any massive secret. I made it through my senior year on a real wing and a prayer." She took a deep breath. "David and I were married in June, and Jarod was born in August." She stared at him suddenly, defiantly. "Just like Sandy. Sandy and Jarod. And that's why I know how hard it's going to be for the two of them."

Dan leaned toward her. He took her champagne glass and set it down, then took both her hands in his. "Kelly, you stayed married, didn't you?"

"Yes, but—"

"Kelly, people should never get married because of a child. There are options. More today than you had. If Sandy had become pregnant by the man in the moon and wanted to keep the baby, I would have stood beside her all the way, whether the boy did or not. But Jarod loves her. I believe that completely. And she loves him. They may be young, and hell, yes, it's going to be tough. But love will keep them together. Your life might have been hard, but, Kelly, you two beat the odds. Hell, I had everything in my corner—and we didn't make it. *You did*. I think that Sandy and Jarod will make it, too."

She smiled wistfully at him. "Think so?"

He brought her hands to his lips and kissed both palms. "I know so. And guess what?"

"What?"

"I think their parents are going to make it, too."

Chapter 10

There were at least fifty people on the ghost tour that night. It was something Kelly had done a dozen times, but she loved it every time. It was really called "Harpers Ferry Myths and Legends," and the proprietress was a marvelous storyteller who didn't swear that ghosts existed, but instead merely pointed out the unusual occurrences that had befallen the city.

There was John Brown, of course. John Brown's raid had made Harpers Ferry famous for generations to come. Kelly linked an arm through Dan's and smiled while they listened to the tale of the old gentleman who periodically arrived in the park, and walked around dressed in nineteenth-century apparel. The rangers all thought he was an actor—the visitors all thought he was a ranger.

He would pose with the visitors, but his image would never come out in the pictures they took. Dozens and dozens of those pictures had been sent to

Washington by amazed visitors—people convinced that John Brown's ghost had returned to the scene of his capture.

Then there were those who thought that the ghost of Mrs. Harper still floated through the top floor of her house. Her husband had told her to bury the family silver, and she had done so. Then she had fallen from a ladder to her death, and some thought that she was still keeping her eye on the buried family treasure—a treasure that had never been found.

The night was beautiful. Dark, with scattered clouds. The spring air swept around them. They were with the group, but in a way Kelly felt that they had never been more alone.

They climbed the steps to the church and heard about the priest who had returned to haunt his parish. Dan asked Kelly in a whisper if this was where the kids were going to be married, and she smiled and nodded. He told her that it was beautiful and traditional, and she was surprised at how glad she was that he liked it.

They went on walking the old streets, and the tales covered the days of bootlegging and revenuers. Dan enjoyed himself thoroughly, and that made Kelly very happy, too.

When the tour was over and people began to disperse, they stood on the dark, deserted street together, alone, holding hands, gazing at each other.

"You liked it?"

"It was wonderful."

"Even to a historian?"

"Especially to a historian."

"You like this place?"

"I love this place. It's nice at night. It's as if the entire world belongs to us, and only us, right now."

"Yes, it is, isn't it?" Kelly murmured. They were standing in back of the old Harper House. The cemetery hill, the Catholic church and the ruins of the Episcopal church were rising behind them, and it was as if that ancient darkness swept around them in a strange blessing. Below them were the river and the main street. By day the costumed rangers would be giving demonstrations on firearms or blacksmithing or day-to-day life in the nineteenth century, but by night it was just an old street, quiet and dark, with a cool breeze that felt like a blessing to Kelly. She wondered if she wasn't actually a part of the place, West Virginia born and bred, a part of the valley and the mountain, and needing their blessing to take the final step.

Fantasy, she warned herself. She spent too much time in a fantasy world of dragons and fairies and elves and knights on white chargers. She loved the old mountain tales, and she loved the ghost stories, and she had to warn herself again that romance and love and a relationship had to be much more than a delightful warm feeling when they walked beneath the stars....

It is, she told herself firmly. Much more.

They came to Dan's car, and he slid into the driver's seat, then looked at her with a grin. "I don't have the faintest idea where we're going."

"Oh!"

Kelly gave him directions through the park to the highway and over the border. They actually drove through three states, but it took barely fifteen minutes, and in another five they were halfway up the mountain, parking the car beside the stream.

"It's dark out here," Dan said.

"Very!" Kelly agreed with a grin. She scampered out of the car, up the walk and into the cabin, thinking wryly that she hoped Jarod had kept the place clean.

He had.

It was just a rough-hewn, one-room cabin, the only addition being the bathroom. The fireplace took up almost an entire wall, and Kelly was delighted to see that Jarod had stacked plenty of wood. The spring night was just cool enough to call for a beautiful fire.

Dan came in with the suitcase she had packed and set it by the counter that separated the kitchen area from the rest of the room. He gazed around at the comfortable sofa and chairs, at the Indian rug in front of the fireplace, and the warm burnt-orange and brown curtains over the windows. Kelly watched him anxiously. His hands were on his hips as he studied the place for a long and careful moment, then turned to her. She hoped desperately that he didn't think it was just a little nothing of a place she had dragged him to when a motel would have been just fine.

"It's wonderful," he told her, moving to her, dropping his hands on her shoulders and touching her mouth with his. "It's the warmest place I've ever been."

She smiled, relieved, and lowered her eyes from his, stepping past him quickly to pick up the suitcase and heave it up on the counter.

"What . . . ?" Dan murmured with a frown.

But by then Kelly had opened the monstrosity to display her heavy wares: a stick of pepperoni, several cheeses, crackers and a vintage red wine.

"Dynamite." Dan laughed. He caught her hands and drew her against his chest. "Perfect. I'll make the fire if you'll cut the pepperoni and pour the wine."

She nodded. She didn't seem to be able to do or say anything else for the moment. He pulled her more tightly against him, and all she could see was the dark fire in his eyes, all she could feel was the way that fire penetrated into her being, making her shiver when she wasn't cold, making her yearn for the hardness of his body. She gazed at him with something like wonder; she had never thought she could feel this way. This wasn't a fantasy. This was real life turning into magic. His touch could make her tremble, melt, yearn to join him in love.

She stared at him, touched his cheek softly, drew lines against the strong planes of his face. He caught her hand, returning her stare seriously, intently.

"I won't be able to make the fire."

"I think you've already made it," she murmured.

He didn't reply. She saw a shadow fall over his face, something taut and tense and older even than the mountain, something that sent a thrill racing up her spine. She felt his hands on the zipper of her dress, and heard the rasping sound it made as it skipped and skimmed over nerves already alive and vibrant. She felt the fabric slide down against her flesh. And then she didn't notice anything at all. The dress had fallen to the floor, and she carelessly kicked it away.

She wondered at his intentions for a moment when he lowered himself to his knees, and then she felt like Cinderella, discovered by her prince, except that this prince had knelt down before her to remove her shoes, rather than to bestow a slipper. She braced herself against his shoulders; then her fingers tightened, as his hands slid along her thighs to the top of her stockings. She caught her breath and cast her head back, dazed by the rising sensations inside her.

He remained kneeling before her, and she realized that she had never known what it was to feel so adored. At first she felt strong and inordinately pleased at her power over his desires, and then incredibly weak, when he touched her so deeply with his caress, that she thought she would fall.

He wouldn't let her fall. Not fall, nor escape. Nor do anything other than receive. His kiss, his touch, his love...

He stroked her with a heat and tenderness that filled her until she had no will of her own. He swept her again and again to the brink, eased her down, swept her up and up and...over.

Panting, gasping, she stared down in amazement, slightly embarrassed. He had been so...intimate, and she was already quivering, drenched....

"You—you shouldn't—" she gasped.

"Why not?"

"Well, I—I—"

He stood and swept her into his arms, and she buried her face against his chest and whispered, "You know why."

"I know that you're wonderful," he told her, walking swiftly.

He carried her to one of the chairs and set her there. Again she felt tremors, ripples, a quivering inside. She heard the rasp of a zipper and, oh, what a sound could do....

She felt it all over again. The warmth, the soaring, the floating, the needing, the rhythm that went on and on, the throbbing need for him.

She rested her cheek against his shoulder, damp, gasping, savoring his body against her, inside her. He filled her with a staggering pleasure, hot and alive and full. She kneaded his shoulders and back, and felt the fabric of his shirt. Deliriously, she wanted to rip it to shreds. Instead she unbuttoned it slowly, shuddered and touched the bare flesh of his chest, then gripped his shoulders and stared into his eyes.

They were dark with hunger, his features taut, straining, almost grim. His eyes closed, and he moved within her, one final thrust, exquisite in the volatile pleasure it gave them both....

They clung together for a moment, panting. Then he raised his head, his eyes alight with amusement, and she flushed again.

"I thought you said you shouldn't?" he teased her.

"Well, I didn't think..." she began primly, but she lowered her lashes at the sound of his laughter.

"Don't worry, okay?" he murmured, then picked her up again and collapsed into the chair with her on his lap. He kissed her lightly and mussed her hair, and as the seconds elapsed she began to feel a different warmth, the same warmth that she had felt in town, when the tour had ended and the darkness had closed around them like a blessing. I love you, she thought again with awe. She didn't say it out loud; it was a frightening thought, deep and dark and true. It wasn't the lovemaking—although making love with him was so wonderful that she still couldn't believe it. But more than that, it was the warmth, the pleasure she felt just in holding his hand, in sitting across the table from him, in listening to him talk, in watching the stars reflected in his eyes.

"I—I have to get dressed," she murmured. "I'm supposed to be cutting pepperoni."

"Don't you dare get dressed," he whispered, nibbling at her ear.

"Dan..."

"I'm going to build the fire," he promised. "The real one."

"Hmm. That felt pretty real to me," Kelly said.

He chuckled softly. "A fire in the hearth. One that we can curl up in front of up here on your beautiful mountain."

She blushed happily, her arms wrapped around his shoulders. "Do you like it? Really?"

"I love it. Really."

"Wait until you see the deer here. They're extraordinary. They're the tamest, sweetest, most gorgeous creatures you'll ever see. I'll bet we can even find them tonight! They'll come to the light—"

"Whoa! I don't—"

"You don't want to see my deer?" she interrupted, crestfallen.

"I'm dying to see your deer. I swear. Just not—not tonight."

"Oh." She started to edge from his lap, but he pulled her back, kissed her deeply and stared into her eyes. "Tonight—" He kissed her once again "—tonight...I want just us. Here. Together, alone."

She returned his kiss and stared at him, feeling awed again. She smiled weakly and started to move. "Really, I have to get dressed and cut the pepperoni."

"Really. The pepperoni will taste a million times better if you cut it...undressed."

Kelly laughed. "You're terrible! And you're not being fair. You're still dressed. Well, sort of, anyway!"

"I'll strip," he swore solemnly. "Right now. Faster than a jackrabbit."

Kelly couldn't help but laugh again. "Dan, honest, you have no modesty."

"No false modesty, my love," he teased. "Really, why did you invite me here?"

"To feed the deer?"

"Not to feed the damn deer—but I will, I will, I swear, I'll feed those deer. Tomorrow. Not tonight. I want to wallow in decadence tonight, okay?"

He slid his loafers off while she was still on his lap. Then, still holding her tightly against his chest, he shed his shirt with a speed that left her gasping and laughing.

Then he stood abruptly, deposited her on her feet and bent over to shimmy out of his jeans—pausing only to glance up at her with a truly diabolical smile.

"Want to help?"

"Help yourself!" She laughed, but she couldn't keep herself from wrapping her arms around her chest. It wasn't easy for her to be totally uninhibited—yet.

Then she turned and raced for the bathroom. She started a quick shower and shivered beneath the cold water, hopping out quickly. Then she grabbed one of the huge white towels off the bar and wrapped herself up in it.

When she walked back out Dan was naked, comfortably hunched down while he set the logs and started the fire. He sat back with satisfaction, whistling a tune, smiling with smug complacency, and merely arching a brow while she strutted by defiantly in her towel.

"No fair," he charged. But then he shrugged and sat on the rug, edging back to lean against the sofa. Kelly poured out two glasses of wine, then dug around under the sink for a cutting board and started on the cheese. When she was done with that she turned her attention to the pepperoni. Her fingers were shaking. She paused and saw the top of Dan's head. She smiled to herself, then set the knife down on the board and carried them both out to him. "You cut, I'll get the wine."

She went back for the wine. He didn't start working right away, though. Instead he went to the closet and with a perfect instinct, procured an armful of pillows and her feather comforter. By the time she had picked up the wineglasses he had created a marvelous little nest in front of the fire. *Then* he began to cut the pepperoni.

Kelly came over with the wine. He paused long enough to look up at her, and she cast him a very suspicious stare.

He smiled serenely and took the wine from her. She started to curl down beside him, then gasped slightly, because he had taken her towel with a little tug.

She smacked his arm and he grunted, warning her that if she wasn't careful he would wind up cutting more than pepperoni. Kelly told him laughingly that he probably deserved just that. When he gazed at her in wounded outrage, she laughed again, winding herself into the comforter and onto his lap.

"You're too good at this," she told him.

He arched a brow. "I beg your pardon? I'm doing my very best for you, madam!"

"You know what I mean!"

"Do I?"

"This!" Kelly waved an arm. "It's my cabin, but you homed right in on the blanket and the pillows."

He stuck a piece of pepperoni into her mouth. "There's only one closet."

Kelly quickly ate the pepperoni, then sipped the wine he handed her. As she leaned over to set the glass on the floor, she studied Dan as he ate—as he watched her watching him. She loved him so much. Everything about him. The way his dark hair fell across his forehead, the high bones of his cheeks, the slant of his nose, the little lines scrawled beside his eyes, the deep tan that attested to the fact that he loved the great outdoors of the present as much as he loved the past.

In fact, she loved the way his whole body was bronzed—except for the whiteness of his rump!

Other women had probably loved him just as much before her, she reflected.

"Out with it," he said.

She shrugged. "I was just thinking about you."

"Were you?"

"Hmm. According to the kids, I should be wary."

"Why?"

"Well, their theory is that you've 'loved 'em and left 'em.'"

"Oh? And how well do they know me?"

"I should think your daughter knows you quite well."

"Great. The little minx has been gossiping about me."

"Well..." Kelly lightly tapped his chest. "I did hear that you...had been around. And now, seeing you in action, well, you *are* something of an expert."

"I try."

Kelly flushed at his brash stare. "That's not what I meant."

"I thought those were cries of joy issuing from your lips!" he exclaimed. "And now I discover that they were complaints."

"Daniel!"

"It's not Daniel. It's Dante."

"Dante! Who names their child Dante?" Kelly laughed.

He shrugged. "My parents. They loved the name. Dante's *Inferno*, and all that."

"You're twisting everything I say—"

"I can't help it. Daniel isn't my name. Dante is."

"Oh! Shut up before I pour wine over your head!"

"You wouldn't."

"I would."

"Then I would have to retaliate by pouring it over your entire body. And then . . . licking it off. Bit by delicious bit."

"Seriously—"

"Oh, I'm dead serious."

"Quit it!" Kelly begged, laughing. "Seriously, how many affairs have you had?"

He paused, frowning slightly, watching her. "Seriously, Kelly, I don't know. I think it would have been rude to keep a scorecard, don't you?"

She picked up her wine, lowering her eyes. Suddenly she didn't like the way he was watching her; it made her uncomfortable about the way she was feeling. She was falling in love with him, but he . . . Who knew what—if anything—he felt for her. "Kelly." He pulled her cheek against his chest, talking softly. "Kelly, I think that Sandy would have liked me to have been serious a few times. She's got a great heart; she's been good to almost everyone I have ever dated. I just never fell in love before. Sandy thinks that I'm hung up because of her mother. I'm not. I even understand—a little bit, I think. It never bothered me that she left me; it killed me that she left Sandy. But she wanted something else out of life. I was drafted, and she was alone. When we were together, we fought. She was so convinced that I was running around when I was away that she almost drove me to it. I think maybe we were destined for divorce. But I'm not harboring any strange phobias because of it.''

Love...

I never fell in love before....

That was what he'd said. Did that mean he was in love now?

Kelly pulled away and took a hasty sip of her wine. Then she looked at him. It was as if she had no choice. His eyes willed her to do so. His eyes, deep and dark and penetrating...

"This is your first affair, isn't it?'' he asked her bluntly. "Your first affair since your husband died. And that,'' he added softly, "was a pretty long time ago.''

She was compelled to nod, to be honest. She badly needed another sip of wine.

But just as she drank, Dan laughed, then bundled her into his arms with enthusiasm. Her glass jiggled, and droplets of rich, red wine spilled all over.

"Wow,'' he teased. "I don't even have to throw it all over you. You just did that yourself!''

"Dan!''

I never fell in love before....

They were the most beautiful words she had ever heard, and they made her laugh with delight. Laugh and laugh until he took the glass from her, stretched her out, manipulating her like a cherished instrument, ready to be played.

She felt his kisses, burning, sweet and hot, against her shoulder, her mouth, her collarbone. Her breasts and her ribs and her waist and . . .

"I didn't spill any wine there!"

"I know."

"Oh . . ."

They made love.

Again and again . . .

And again.

Before the fire, the blaze casting beautiful gilded patterns against their skin. It was a night of discovery. As long as she lived, Kelly would remember kneeling while he knelt, touching his shoulders, drawing her fingers across his skin, then leaning over and pressing her lips along the same path. Dan patiently allowed her all her whimsy, allowed her to become someone bolder, someone surer. Not just eager, but intense. Not just giving, but receiving.

In the end Kelly had no desire to make up the bed. She was too exhausted, too comfortable there before the fire. It was dying now, glowing softly, and she began to doze after the perfection of their lovemaking.

Dan nudged her.

"I can't," she groaned. "I really can't."

He laughed. "I was going to ask if you have another blanket in there. Then you can keep your cute little tush on the comforter and I can put something else over us."

"Hmm," Kelly murmured lazily. "You must be slipping. There's a whole pile of blankets in the closet."

She was so tired she could barely speak, barely open her eyes. She felt him stand, heard him pad over to the closet.

She must have dozed then, if only for a few seconds. She came awake and realized that he hadn't come back. And yet he was still there. Still in the cabin. She knew that with a special sixth sense. She knew her love; she knew when he stood, when he walked, when he moved....

But he wasn't moving. And she could feel something heavy in the air, an omen, a portent.

Frowning, Kelly struggled to sit up. "Dan?" He didn't answer, and she turned around to see him.

He was standing there, silent, still, his expression like a thundercloud. He was holding something and staring at it. Kelly edged away nervously, her hand fluttering to her throat. "Dan?"

He looked at her at last, but he didn't say anything. "Dan, what...?"

Suddenly he was moving toward her shaking something in front of her face. Something white and lacy.

Sandy's bra, Kelly realized. Damn them! Damn the two of them. They hadn't only managed to get Sandy pregnant—they'd managed to leave half their clothing behind.

"Do you know what this is?" Dan demanded heatedly.

"A bra," she said dully. "You don't need to be Einstein to answer that one."

"No, not *a* bra!" he stormed at her. "Sandy's bra! This whole thing was your fault!"

"My fault!" Kelly shrieked.

"Yes! The rest of the kids out there at least have to go through a little effort! Get out of the house, rent a hotel room, suffer it out in the car! Effort? Jarod? Oh no! His mother provides him with a cozy, isolated place. Not only a nice soft bed—but clean sheets, too!"

"Oh!" Kelly screeched, enraged in turn. She wasn't tired anymore. She stood and strode about furiously in the darkness, desperate to find her clothing. To her horror, he trailed after her, still talking.

"You led them right to it!"

"*I led them right to it?* You're sick, Marquette, do you know that? What do you think—that I dragged Sandy up here? That I sent her an engraved invitation?"

She found her panties and stumbled into them, then her slip. Bending down along with her, he picked up her bra and her dress and her shoes.

"Jarod sure as hell invited her up!"

"She could have said no!"

"She was innocent!"

"She probably seduced him!"

"Oh, yeah? I suppose he invited her up here just like you invited me up here—innocently. To watch the deer! Oh, yeah, let's go up to my mother's cabin. It has a super bed, a fridge, you name it. Let's go up to this little love nest and feed the damn deer! Sure!"

"Oh!" Kelly exclaimed again, staring at him furiously. It was all she could think of in her rage. Then she noticed her dress and shoes and lacy bit of underwear in his hand and grabbed them from him.

"Do you know what this is, Sherlock? My bra! So give it to me!"

Fumbling, she managed to shimmy into the rest of her clothing. He must really have been floored by his discovery of the "scene of the crime." Apparently he hadn't even noticed that she was dressing.

"What the hell do you think you're doing?"

"Leaving!" Kelly retorted.

"In the middle of the night? In the middle of nowhere?"

"You guessed it, Sherlock."

"Oh, no, you're not!"

"Oh, yes, I am!"

She had slammed her way out the front door before he had regrouped enough to think to stop her. Kelly smiled grimly, wishing she'd taken his keys—but willing to walk down the mountain. It was her mountain; she knew it like the back of her hand. And she would have a good head start on him. He couldn't come rushing out stark naked. He would have to take the time to get his pants on.

As soon as she started down the path that would lead her toward the stream and the trail that went all the way down to the highway, an uneasy sensation stirred right at the base of her spine. She heard a rustling in the bushes.

It's a deer, Kelly, she told herself. A squirrel.

But it wasn't an animal. Not the four-footed variety, at any rate. She knew it. Just knew it. Sheer, blinding, horrible instinct told her that there was someone behind her. Someone evil. Someone who meant to slink through the darkness and brush and attack her, assault her.

She inhaled, desperate to scream. But who would hear her? How far had she come? Would Dan reach her—in time?

She turned; she could keep her back to the danger no longer. And she saw them. Those eyes. Those same horrible eyes, gleaming in the darkness. Eyes that had stared at her before. Eyes that were filled with pure malice and menace...

There was enough light for her to see that they belonged to a man. Medium height, husky build. Reaching for her now in the darkness.

She screamed at last, loud and long and shrill. Then, when he was just about to touch her, he suddenly fell instead.

Something was on top of him. Something bronze, except for a little patch of white. On the rump.

Dan.

Of all the deplorable—absolutely fantastic!—gall.

He hadn't bothered with his jeans, or even his briefs! He had just waltzed out after her—naked as a jaybird, and now he was embroiled in a horrible fight—for her.

She screamed again. With the darkness, she could hear the blows falling, but she didn't have the faintest idea what was happening.

"Oh, God!"

"Kelly!"

"Dan! That must be him! The Peeper! The guy they're looking for. And oh, God, Dan! It was him! The other night, staring in at me..."

He was there, her naked savior, taking her into his arms. Trembling, shaking, she fell into them.

"Shh, Kelly, it's all right."

"He was up here! He was probably trying to break into the cabin for food, for—"

"Kelly, it's all right!"

"Oh..."

"He's unconscious. We've got to call the police."

She nodded, trembling.

"You all right?"

"I will be. Dan?"

"What?"

"Please, uh, put your jeans back on while I dial, huh?"

"Sure, kid, sure," He tapped her chin with his knuckles, and they went back to the cabin together, Dan dragging their captive along.

Chapter 11

The good news was that they had caught the Peeper.

The bad news—to Kelly's way of thinking—was that the story of his capture was plastered over the front pages of newspapers as far away as D.C. and Knoxville.

Thank God Dan had gotten into his jeans before the police had come!

Still, in black and white, for all the world to see, the papers reported that she and Dan had been in the cabin on the mountain. The police had been called at 3:48 a.m. and had arrived to find the Peeper still unconscious, with Mr. Dante Marquette and Mrs. Kelly McGraw standing guard over the subject.

It would have been impossible to tell Jarod that they had driven to the cabin at 3:48 a.m. to feed the deer.

He and Sandy came back around eleven to find Kelly, Dan and Reeves sipping coffee in Dan's living room. Jarod had burst in like a small tornado, with

Sandy in his wake, waving a newspaper in front of him.

"Mom!"

He raced over to her and gave her one of his massive hugs, the kind that she was afraid would break her one day. She was gratified and relieved—at least his first thought was still to assure himself that she was all right.

Sandy gave her the next hug, a much gentler one. "I would have been just terrified. Thank God they caught that awful man, and thank God he's locked up again. I'm so glad you and Dad were together. . . ." Then she kissed and hugged her father, then told him that he was a hero.

Dan cleared his throat and actually blushed, then told Sandy not to be ridiculous, that he had just been there, and he had gotten the first good slug in.

"Ohhh . . . Kelly! I would have been so scared! I'd probably have had a heart attack!" Sandy insisted.

"Tea, Sandra? Mr. McGraw?" Reeves interrupted.

"Coffee for me, Reeves, thanks," Jarod said, and Kelly realized that already her son was changing, a belligerent expression crossing his handsome young face. She didn't like the way he was looking at her, and liked the way he was looking at Dan even less.

She decided not to confront him and to respond to Sandy's comment instead. "Sandy, I really didn't have time to be frightened. I heard him behind me, and then your dad was on top of him," she said.

Jarod had moved to the window, hands clasped behind his back, staring intently out at the scenery. He turned to Kelly with a curious smile. "What were you doing out on that path at three in the morning, Mom?"

Kelly hardened her features and her heart and stared at him coolly. "Walking, Jarod."

"So you two were up at the cabin together, huh?"

"Yes, Jarod—" Kelly began, but Dan was suddenly up, sweeping past her, and she began to remember exactly why she had been on that path.

"Yes, we were up at the cabin, Jarod," he said easily, conversationally, crossing his arms over his chest. "And do you really want to know what your mother was doing on that path?"

Kelly watched Jarod's knuckles go white. "Yes, I do!" he announced defiantly, his pulse beating at the base of his throat.

"Jarod!" Sandy said in alarm, racing over toward him. She tried to calm him down, to grab his hand, but he wouldn't let her.

Even Dan said, "Stay out of this, Sandy."

"Now wait a minute—" Kelly began.

"You, too, Mom!" Jarod snapped.

It wasn't that she intended to listen to him; it was pure surprise that kept Kelly standing there, her mouth agape.

"I'll tell you what she was doing on the path!" Dan seemed to roar with the power of a locomotive. "She was walking out on me. And do you want to know *why* she was walking out on me?"

"Why?" Jarod asked a bit more slowly and warily.

"We were arguing, Jarod. It's funny. The truth had just slapped me in the face, I mean, I knew it—I think parents just know things sometimes that they don't exactly want to see. But there I was, picking up pieces of my daughter's underwear, and something about it just made me snap. I knew what you two had done, but I hadn't known where you had done it, and suddenly I was forced to stare it all in the face. Hell! You two couldn't even get dressed after! So I blamed your mother, Jarod. Blamed her for having the cabin. It wasn't fair, but I wasn't being particularly rational. And she was naturally furious, so she walked out on me. In the middle of the night. I tried to catch her, to apologize. That's the full explanation, Jarod. But do you know what, son? I think that if you have any sense at all in that brain of yours, you won't mention that cabin to me again. Or ask either one of us what we were doing in it."

Jarod stared at him for a long, long time without answering, but his fists kept clenching and unclenching. Suddenly he turned to stare at Kelly. "Mother, I'm leaving. Are you coming?"

"Jarod, I think that—"

"I think you're acting like a spoiled brat and that you'd better watch your step with me, young man," Dan warned.

"Watch my step!" Jarod growled. "We've been through this before. I love Sandy. There's a big difference." He stared at Kelly again. "A real big difference."

"Jarod, really!" Kelly snapped, stunned and incredulous that he would behave this way. "Jarod, I'm your mother! You're not out of high school, and I'm thirty-five. I've raised you, and I have the right—"

"It has nothing to do with rights, Mother. It has to do with him. Don't you see? It's humiliating. He doesn't want anything but—it's just like being his whore."

There was a deathly silence. Kelly was too amazed to talk; Sandy—and Dan—seemed to be in shock.

Jarod turned and stormed out of the house, slamming the door in his wake.

"I'm going to kill him!" Dan swore suddenly. "Take him apart limb by obnoxious limb—"

"Dad, no!" Sandy cried. "Dad, he really doesn't mean anything," she said desperately, running to her father and clutching his arm, holding it tightly—barely restraining him. He stared at her. "Dad, please! Let me talk to him. He's upset; he'll apologize!"

She tried to smile at them both, her face ashen. "Please!" she whispered, and she stared at Kelly. "Please!"

Kelly still couldn't move. She felt frozen. She could only watch as Sandy went racing out after Jarod.

Through the huge window, Kelly and Dan could see them clearly; Sandy trying to soothe him; Jarod shaking off her desperate grip on his shoulder.

Then Dan was suddenly in motion. He started toward the door. Every maternal instinct in Kelly came surging to the fore, and she raced after him.

She was so small and he was so big that for an instant it was as if he didn't know that she had caught hold of him, that she was hanging on his arm.

"Dan!"

He kept walking.

"Dan!"

He stopped and stared down at her.

"Dan!" Kelly screamed a third time.

"I won't have her out there like that! Whining and pleading with that obnoxious, overgrown brat!"

"Dan, damn you, she's going to marry him! She's carrying his child, and he's my son! *My son!*"

"And you didn't do a damn thing to shut him up!" he reminded her contemptuously.

Kelly jerked away from him as if he had burned her, and she stared at her hands as if they had been dirtied.

"That's right, Marquette, I didn't. Like I said, he's my son. That relationship is between the two of us. Even if he is an obnoxious brat, he's being protective. And if you so much as go near him, I'll never speak to you again."

"Kelly, listen to you! You're defending his behavior!"

"Damn right," she said, and she backed away. She saw her purse, lying on the sofa. She picked it up and marched regally toward the door.

Outside, she went sailing by Jarod and Sandy, who stared after her in silence.

Kelly couldn't see what went on behind her. She only knew that a second later Jarod had caught up with her. That he was upset, anxious. He opened the passenger door and ushered her in, then moved around to the driver's seat.

They drove home in an awful and absolute silence.

"Mom..." Jarod began once he had parked the car in front of the house.

But Kelly had nothing to say to him. She slammed the car door and started for the house.

He followed. "Mother! Don't you see? Don't you understand? He's all right as a man. As a father-in-law. He likes mountains and streams and fishing and football. And women! Mom, I know you! I've known you all my life—"

Still silent, Kelly twisted the key in the front door and stepped inside.

Jarod was right on her tail. "I've known you all my life, right?"

Kelly noticed that there were tears brimming in his blue eyes. They didn't touch her. Nothing seemed to touch her at that moment. Jarod had created a schism, and then Jarod had needed her, and Dan—damn him!—had come on like gangbusters, and Kelly had really had no choice but to stand up for Jarod.

And now Jarod...

"The cabin, Mom!" he exclaimed in sudden fury, clenching his hands at his sides. "How could you? How could you go up there with that man and sell out?"

Kelly slapped him. Hard. And then, even as he clutched his cheek in astonishment, she backed him up against the staircase. "I own that cabin, Jarod; you don't! And without my knowing a damn thing about it, you brought that man's daughter—his innocent, underaged daughter!—up there. And she's pregnant. And he went out of his way and I went out of my way to try to smooth the way for you. We're both trying to see things rationally, and we're both willing to help with whatever decisions the two of you make—and you repay me like this? Jarod..."

There were tears in his eyes. Real tears. "It was my father's cabin!" he shouted back. "My father's cabin! It was all right for me to be there! It was all right for me to be with a girl there. It wasn't all right for you! You betrayed him. I was conceived there! It was my father's place!"

Kelly stopped short, filled with confusion, dizziness and misery. "Jarod, I haven't betrayed your father! Your father is dead."

Jarod suddenly sank down on the bottom step, holding his head between his hands. "It was Dad's cabin," he repeated softly.

Kelly sank down beside him, slipping an arm around his broad shoulders. "Jarod, I loved your father, through thick and thin. A lot of things were very hard, and we made it anyway. But, Jarod, he's gone. I miss him, you miss him, but I've been alone a long, long time!"

He wasn't convinced. He looked up at her bitterly again. "So you hopped into bed with Marquette the first chance you got."

Her hand itched to slap him again. "Damn you, Jarod! I do not believe this! You go out and get that poor girl pregnant, then have the nerve to tell me what I can and can't do. I will not have it!"

She stood, a tangle of tension and emotion. She started up the stairway, unaware that he had stood up, too, that he was watching her with the tears, the uncertainty, brimming in his eyes once more.

"Mother! Don't you understand! I love Sandy! Dad loved you; you loved Dad!"

She swung around, still incensed. "No, Jarod, I guess I just don't understand anything. And all I want you to know is this—if I decide to dance naked on the front lawn, that's exactly what I'm going to do. And I don't need your permission to do it! Whatever the hell it was—love or lust—it was of my choosing. I'm old enough to choose, Jarod, and you're not! I don't have anything else to say on the matter, and quite frankly, Jarod, I really don't want to talk to you right now! Excuse me, please!"

She went up to her room, and this time she didn't even have the energy to slam her door. She just closed it, then locked it.

She sat down on her bed and lifted her hands helplessly, then started to cry. She hated them. Both of them! How dare Jarod call her names? How dare he think that he could dictate to her?

And Dan! What the hell was the matter with him? Couldn't he understand that Jarod would naturally be upset? Couldn't he have a little patience, a little empathy? Sandy didn't remember her mother. Jarod *did* remember his father. And he was a sensitive young man; maybe something about the cabin really was sacred to him.

She stopped crying and lay back on her bed, staring up at the ceiling. Damn, damn, damn Dan! What would have happened if they hadn't been fighting to begin with? The cabin would have been locked; the Peeper might just have gone on his way.

And still be on the loose, Kelly reminded herself. Dangerous and on the loose, but now he was back behind bars.

A lot of women would be safe. Her happiness was certainly a small price to pay, wasn't it?

She and Dan hadn't even mentioned their fight after the police had arrived. It had seemed too petty. The police had taken the Peeper away, and she and Dan had gone back to his house, where Reeves had made them a couple of good stiff Scotches.

They had sat on the couch and drunk them together. A pair, a team, a couple. His arm had remained around her all the night; she had dozed with her head against his shoulder, and it had been so nice. In good times and in bad. That was what love was all about, wasn't it? Laughing together, knowing fear together. Dan's wild anger had sent him hurtling against an unknown danger because she was being threatened.

In the same way, she had stood up for Jarod, because she loved him—and because Dan had threatened him.

Except that she loved Dan, too. Jarod didn't know that, couldn't see it, and she was afraid to tell him. She had been coming to trust Dan, to believe in him, to believe that he loved her, too, that their relationship was more than an affair.

And now...

Maybe he would call her. Maybe he would apologize. He couldn't disappear; he couldn't walk out of her life. They would have to see each other again, because of the kids. Jarod and Sandy were still going to get married.

Kelly sighed, she was exhausted. She'd barely had an hour's sleep, and her crying jag had exhausted her further. Kelly sighed softly again, and fell to sleep.

Dan walked out into the backyard, where the air was cool and the trees offered some shade, a place where he could try to curb the awful heat of his temper. He walked, because walking would burn steam; he threw rocks, because tossing them used up the tension in his muscles.

He stared up at the sky—and he talked to it.

"What in God's name is the matter with her? After what Jarod did, how dare he preach to us? He's crazy. That boy took my baby..."

He drew a long breath, then exhaled slowly. He was crazy to keep getting upset about Sandy. He had accepted her pregnancy; he had accepted Jarod. They were going to get married; it was going to be all right.

He had been wrong to get upset again at the cabin because he had discovered Sandy's underwear, but it had been natural. A man shouldn't have to discover the scene of his daughter's loss of innocence, but he'd had no right to take it out on Kelly, and he knew it.

But this...

"That kid deserves a good smack on the butt!" he told the sky. That kid... That kid was going to be his son-in-law. The father of his grandchild. Lord, what a mess.

"She'll call me," he murmured, sitting down and plucking a piece of grass. He chewed on it and reflected. Yes, Kelly would call him. She would call him because she knew damn well that she had been wrong, that Jarod had been way out of line. Jarod was going to have to come to him and apologize—if he ever wanted to see Sandy again. And once he and Jarod got everything straightened out, Kelly would have to call him.

Because he was right.

He closed his eyes. He wanted to see her. He wanted her back. Sitting on the sofa, handing him a cup of coffee. Staring out the window, laughing, talking, just being with him.

He wanted to be with her. Holding hands across the table at a restaurant. Her eyes bright and excited, and staring into his. Her arm looped through his as she dragged him along.

Up at the cabin...

At the cabin, where they had touched and the blaze had begun. It had been an inferno, a thirst that had to be quenched. And her laughter. That was so important and precious to them, being together after the loving, holding each other....

I love you, Kelly McGraw, he thought, and he stared ahead at nothing, chewing his piece of grass. I love you, and I want you, and I'm...

"I'm sorry!" he swore aloud, rising. But as much as he wanted her, as much as he wanted to hear her voice, he'd be damned if he was going to call her and apologize and tell her, sure, let her son run around acting as if their being together was something dirty and illicit. If Jarod had been anyone else in the world and he had called Kelly a whore, Dan would have decked him.

But he *was* her son....

I miss you! he thought again.

She'll call me! he promised himself. She *would* call, because she was wrong. She had to call.

But Kelly didn't call. She didn't call on Sunday, and she didn't call on Monday. Or Tuesday.

On Wednesday Dan discovered that Sandy had taken his side. She hadn't said a word to Jarod since he had walked away on Sunday.

She wouldn't really talk to Dan about it, but when he asked her if she had seen Kelly, she said no, certainly not, that she hadn't even spoken to Jarod.

"Sandy," he had reminded her softly, "you and Jarod have to straighten this out. Not talking doesn't seem to be the answer. Maybe I should—"

"No!" Sandy interjected fiercely. "No, Dad! Jarod has to grow up! I will not let our situation influence yours again!"

She was gone before Dan could say more.

He spent Thursday and Friday working, then discovered on Saturday that he hadn't really accomplished anything.

He sat and stared out his plate-glass windows, watching the trees and the birds, and he wondered again how things could have come to such a pass.

Someone needed to talk to Jarod. Someone needed to knock some sense into the boy. It should be him—except that both his daughter and the woman he loved were determined that it wouldn't be.

Now his daughter was miserable, he was miserable, Jarod had to be miserable and surely—surely!—Kelly was, too. Unless he had imagined it all. Unless she really didn't love him. Maybe he had been just a diversion to her. The new man in town and all that.

It was ridiculous. The whole situation was ridiculous. And he was making himself crazy thinking about it.

But nothing changed.

The weekend passed. Sandy moped around the house, and so did he. Reeves kept walking around pretending that nothing was wrong, but Dan could tell that even the old gentleman's gentleman was upset.

Dan talked to Sandy again. He reminded her that she and Jarod were planning a future—the rest of their lives—together. That whether he and Jarod were best friends or not really didn't matter, but that whether the two of them got along did.

Dan decided—in silence—that if Jarod didn't come around to see him by the next weekend, he would go find the boy. Sandy couldn't be any more unhappy than she already was, and hell, Kelly wasn't speaking to him anyway. And beyond a doubt, Jarod deserved a good walloping.

To aggravate Dan's feelings of injustice, Sandy was feeling sick, because she was pregnant.

Boy, when I get my hands on you...he vowed silently.

On Wednesday night, everything changed.

Sandy came home nearly hysterical. Dan wasn't there when she came in from school, but he came back to find Reeves frantic, because Sandy had come in crying, slammed into her room, stayed there for a few minutes—then run out. And he didn't know where she was.

Dan went out looking for her. He found her walking toward town and got her into the car, where she promptly burst into tears. Dan decided that he could quite happily take a shotgun to Jarod McGraw.

He took her home, but it was still over an hour before he could get Sandy to talk him. Then Sandy didn't want to shut up.

She walked around the room and ranted and raved and said that Jarod thought he was Mr. Macho and he was a cheat and he was awful and she had made the biggest mistake of her life and she wasn't sure if she even wanted to live. She didn't want the baby, and she didn't want any part of Jarod.

In the end Dan discovered that it was all because Jarod had been talking to a redheaded cheerleader. To his credit, Dan stayed fairly calm. He was convinced that Jarod had purposely tried to make Sandy jealous because Sandy had been giving him the silent treatment.

He calmed her down, then decided that this was the time to find Jarod himself. But when he picked up the phone to call the McGraw house, he stopped. Sandy was already on the line—to Jarod. She sounded cool, sophisticated, regal—the perfect lady.

He hung up. Sandy could clearly handle this one herself.

A few minutes later he heard her hang up. A second after that, the phone rang. Dan picked it up.

"Dan, Mr. Marquette! You can't let her do it! Please, sir, you can't."

"Who is this?" Dan asked, smiling. He knew perfectly well who it was, but the boy deserved to squirm a little.

"Me. Jarod. Sandy is mad at me over some little thing—"

"Jarod, this is not 'some little thing.' Son—"

"I'm sorry!" Jarod exclaimed, "Oh, God, I'm sorry! Sir, you don't understand. I know I offended you, but you see, you've proved my point. You really don't care anything about my mother—"

"We're getting off the real subject here, Jarod, but a son who loves his mother does not refer to her as a whore. And that goes whether you want to consider me Mr. Right or not. And your behavior toward me—"

"Please, I'm sorry! Please—"

"I think you owe your mother the apology."

There was silence for a minute.

"Yes, sir," he said very softly. "Yes, sir, I know that. I owe you both an apology. But Dan—Mr. Marquette—sir! Please, you've got to help me. Sandy is thinking of giving up the baby. She can't do that! That baby is mine, too. She has no right—"

"Maybe she doesn't. Decisions regarding the baby should be made by the two of you." He hesitated. "On this, Jarod, I do agree with you. The baby is yours, as much as it's Sandy's."

"Mr. Marquette, she says that she's going to go take care of the paperwork right now. Please, don't let her leave the house. Not until I get there."

"I'll try."

"I know that she respects you. I know that if you tell her not to leave that house, she won't. Please—"

"Don't beg, Jarod. I don't want you to grovel!"

There was silence. Then Jarod said softly, "What *do* you want, Mr. Marquette?"

"Respect, a right to live my own life, and a right to privacy. And an apology to your mother."

"Yes, sir. I'll—I'll be there in ten minutes."

Dan hung up the phone, smiling. Sandy came out of her room and smiled back at him. Her tears were gone, and she suddenly looked completely serene.

"Dad?"

"Yeah?"

"He's on his way over here, isn't he?"

"Yes."

She flew across the room and threw her arms around him. "I love you, Dad!"

"And you love Jarod, too, huh, baby?"

She nodded, beautiful eyes wide.

"As mad as I've been at Jarod, Sandy, I believe with all my heart that he loves you."

She nodded. Then she smiled. "And you love her, don't you? Kelly. You love Kelly."

"Yeah. I think I do, babe. I think I do."

Chapter 12

She was lying on her bed, one arm cast over her eyes. She should have been downstairs, working. Daryl the Devilish Dragon had only pretended to help Esmeralda the Fairy Queen and now all hell was breaking loose in the kingdom. The White knights were being sent out, but Daryl had imps on his teams, and havoc was in store.

Kelly rolled over and thought about Daryl. She should have made him a frog. Then, at some point, Esmeralda could have looked into those dark eyes, fallen madly in love and then kissed him—and he could have turned into a prince.

"Prince! Hah!"

Yes, she should have been downstairs, working, but she was in a state of absolute panic. Lying on her bed and waiting. Afraid to walk back into the bathroom and look at the vial to see what color the paper strip had turned.

"I can't be!" She whispered the words, and she couldn't help but remember the first time she had whispered them.

She was older now, and supposedly wiser, but all that had done for her was to warn her that saying "I can't be!" couldn't make "not" if she "was."

Stupid, stupid, stupid!

And what are you going to do about it?

She couldn't think about that. She didn't dare.

My God, she thought anyway. I got married once because I had to, and it's the most awful reason in the world. It isn't fair—it really isn't fair—that it should happen twice....

She got up, but she didn't quite make it to the bathroom. She gripped the dresser, because a wave of dizziness seized her, and it had nothing to do with the condition she might or might not be in. What did she mean, she couldn't do it again? What were her choices, her options? And would Dan even think about marrying her? It wasn't the same again. It was eighteen years later, and this was an entirely new game.

She had finally gotten through college; her career was established; she had things going in the right direction now. Jarod and Sandy didn't have any of these things—as of this moment, they didn't even have high school diplomas.

Which was completely beside the point, Kelly thought. They weren't the problem—*she* was. And she wasn't even sure. To be sure, she had to walk into the bathroom and look to see what color the little strip of paper had turned. Then, she reminded herself, she would be sure.

She managed to walk into the bathroom.

"Ahh!" The paper wasn't the color she wanted it to be.

Holding the sink, she sank down to sit on the commode. The test could be wrong. It wasn't foolproof. She could see her doctor, and he could tell her that . . .

She stared at the vial again, frowning. Actually, the paper wasn't any color that it was supposed to be. What did that mean? It wasn't nice and clear, and it wasn't pastel pink.

"I'm not pregnant; I've scared myself into a tizzy," she assured herself.

But what if she was?

She felt crazy. She couldn't think.

"Mom!"

She closed her eyes, vaguely aware of Jarod calling her. She leaned over the sink and splashed cold water against her face.

She was falling apart. The sane thing to do was to give the doctor a call and tell him that the test hadn't turned any particular color and ask what that meant.

"Mother!"

Oh, no, Jarod was there. Right there in her bedroom, and on his way closer.

Was there no escape from this tall, handsome and at one time fairly sane child? First her love life went to pot on his account—once she had finally achieved one—and now he was right on top of her, about to view the results of that love life.

It was just too much. He went out and got a girl pregnant, then dragged her father home to get his mother pregnant. It was laughable, really. Hysterical, that was what it was.

"Mom, I'm going out. I've got to get over to Sandy's. She hasn't spoken to me for over a week. And today all I did was pass the time of day with Brenda and I had Sandy on the phone telling me she wouldn't marry me if I were the last guy on earth. I'm afraid of what—of what she might do."

"Jarod, I don't think that Sandy really wants to do anything about the baby," Kelly managed to tell him. She had to get rid of the little vial. Subtly, before Jarod saw it.

"I'll kill her if she does. I'll wring her neck. I'll—"

"Jarod, I'm sure she didn't mean it. She was trying to make you jealous. Or maybe she wanted you to give her father an apology, which, God knows, he deserves."

"She doesn't have the right!"

"Jarod, damn it, then go talk to her! You said you were leaving, so go!"

He nodded; he was about to turn around. But then he stopped, his eyes widening. "What is that? What are you doing?"

"Nothing."

"That isn't nothing. That's a—a—Mother!"

"Oh, Jarod, please . . ."

"You're pregnant!"

"Jarod—"

"By a man!"

"That's usually the way it happens."

"No, not *a* man—*that* man. Him. Dan. Marquette! Oh, my God! Mom, I warned you!"

"Jarod, I'm not. I just proved that I'm not."

He stared at her, ashen-faced. Fear for what he might do suddenly seized her.

"Jarod, I'm telling you the truth! Now, please, butt out of my affairs, will you? There's nothing to worry about."

"Are you sure?"

"Yes. Positive. Look, Jarod, I'm your mother, so listen to me, please. I'm fine, so will you please give me some privacy? You came running up here all upset about Sandy. I'm not asking you, I'm telling you— and I mean it! Forget about me for the time being. Go over and see Sandy; work out your problems. And don't you dare mention my name—do you understand?"

He stared at her miserably, shaking his head.

"Jarod..."

"I'm going. I'm going to talk Sandy out of a terrible mistake."

"Then do it, will you?" He had to leave; she had to call the doctor and ask him what the test meant.

"Okay, okay!" He gave her a curious smile, and then he was gone.

Kelly listened to his footsteps going down the stairs; then she heard the front door close. She stood up slowly and fought the wave of misery and nausea that assailed her.

With a furious oath she tossed the vial and the paper and everything else involved with the test into the garbage. She kept swearing at herself all the way down the stairs to the kitchen.

How could she have let something like this happen? She? *He!* It was his fault. His stupid fault.

Wasn't he supposed to have said something about protection the very first time?

Kelly reached the kitchen and leaned her forehead against the cool refrigerator door. The very first time they had just stared at each other and said inane things. There had been a dangerous rapist running around outside, and they hadn't even worried about it!

We didn't know, she reminded herself.

Even if they had, it wouldn't have changed anything.

Nothing had mattered; it had been that simple. They had touched, and that had been that.

Who the hell could get pregnant from one lousy night?

Lots of women through the ages, she assured herself sagely. And then she kicked the refrigerator. It wasn't fair! She thought back to high school. Tina Norman had messed around all the time, she'd admitted to all kinds of carelessness, and she'd never been caught! It wasn't fair!

Especially not twice in a lifetime.

Kelly groaned aloud, not because she had hurt her toe—which she had—but because she just couldn't believe her own stupidity. She was thirty-five years old! She couldn't have been foolish enough to get into this situation again!

But she had been. She had wanted him so badly that night. So desperately. It had been magic; it had been the culmination of all her fantasies. He'd swept her right off her feet, and she had adored it—and him.

She smiled a little bitterly. A love affair, easily begun, easily ended. What would it be like if they were still speaking? Would she have told him about her fears? Would she have asked him to hold her hand while she waited for the minutes to pass before she could check on her test?

I'm in love with him, she thought suddenly, and the emotion was both painful and sweet. She asked herself sternly if it wasn't the fact that she was afraid she might be pregnant that made her feel that way. It wasn't. She had been upset; she had been angry; she had been hurt. But she was still in love with him. She was stubborn and he was temperamental, but that didn't change her love.

She finally swung the door open. She needed a good stiff drink. Wrong side. She closed the refrigerator and opened the freezer to get some ice.

A bourbon. She needed straight bourbon. She could have cried, except that she was too old to cry. A drink would take away the pain. It would help her think and plan.

She poured bourbon over ice, her hands shaking. She couldn't do it again. She just couldn't do it again. She couldn't get married because she had to. If there was anything between her and Dan, it had to be allowed to grow. She just couldn't go through another shotgun wedding.

She brought the bourbon to her lips, but she couldn't drink it. If she *was* pregnant, the last thing she should have was a drink.

She had to think. What were her alternatives?

The words shrieked across her mind. Everyone knew the alternatives. She didn't have to marry Dan. She could have the child, then give it up for adoption. Or she could . . .

Oh, get serious. If he ever found out, he'd wring her neck.

Or would he? Maybe he would be relieved. He probably had absolutely no interest in marriage. Maybe he'd even rather have her get rid of the child. If there was a child...

Kelly swallowed sharply. Why was she panicking? She didn't even know if she was pregnant yet. She quickly hastened to the phone and called the doctor's office. His nurse promised that he would call her right back.

To Kelly's surprise and vast relief, he did.

"Dr. Baker here, Kelly. What's the problem?"

"I, uh..." She hesitated for a second, then plunged in. She told him the brand name of the test, and explained about the strange color.

"I get more calls on that darn test," he said. "No, Kelly, you aren't pregnant. If you're late, it's probably because you've worked yourself into a state. In fact, I'll bet you're feeling better already."

She didn't really know what she felt. She was so surprised and relieved that she sank to the floor, holding the receiver.

"Kelly?"

"Yes, I'm here. Thank you."

"Sure thing." He went on to recommend a more reliable test, should she ever want to try it again. Kelly thanked him—dryly, this time—and hung up.

She stayed on the floor for several moments. She was very relieved. Really.

But her lips curled into a soft smile. Maybe she was just a tiny bit disappointed, too.

* * *

It wasn't that he had meant to lie to her; he hadn't. It was just that it was impossible to do as she asked, and with each block that he drove, Jarod felt a greater, more consuming fear—and fury.

Sandy was out front, waiting for him. Jarod was glad that she was alone, but it wouldn't really have mattered. He'd never felt so aggressive and hostile in his life, not even on a football field. He thundered up to Sandy, took both of her hands and drew her roughly against him. "Forget it, do you hear me—"

"Jarod McGraw, I—"

"Sandy, forget it. I mean it. I don't care how mad you get; I don't care what idiotic things you're thinking or feeling. Don't ever, ever even consider such a stupid thing again. Sandy, our wedding is less than two months away. We're going to get married. And we're not going to be playing house. We'll be together for the rest of our lives—and that baby's life, too. I swear, Sandy, that if I even suspect you're thinking such a thing again, I'll drag you out of this house—father or no!—and shackle you to my wrist until that baby is born. Do you understand?"

"Jarod, how dare you!"

"Oh, I dare, Sandy, I promise you!"

"After what you did today, you want to have a child—well, you just go talk to your cheerleading friend about it! That nice, sweet, bouncy little cutie would probably bounce right into—"

"Sandy!"

"What?"

"Sandy..."

He drew her to him and kissed her pouting lips with love and tenderness.

"I don't want anybody's baby but ours. You're going to be my wife, and I love you. You gave me the silent treatment and I tried to make you jealous, and I'm sorry. I love you, Sandy."

"Oh, Jarod..."

She slipped her arms around him, then leaned against him. She felt so happy. The strain between them had been terrible; this felt just like coming home. It was warm and secure and beautiful, and he really loved her. Their future was secure again. And it felt so good just to rest against him....

Except that he distractedly pushed her away, and she almost fell, she was so surprised.

"Where's your father?"

"What?"

"Where's your father?"

"Oh, you want to apologize! He'll be so glad, Jarod. He really likes you, you know—"

"Apologize!" Jarod exclaimed.

Sandy felt her heart sink like lead. No. Not again. She felt ill; she felt her stomach churn.

He'd already pushed past her; he was on his way into the house.

"Jarod!"

She raced after him and caught his arm, but he kept walking. "Dan! Mr. Marquette! *Sir!*"

Sandy shivered slightly as she saw her father come out of his office. He had one brow slightly arched, and his dark eyes were narrowed. Sandy knew her father. She could tell that he hadn't liked the tone of Jarod's voice. Not one bit. And he was going to let Jarod come in for whatever his attack was...and then counter. Counter with such force and speed that Jarod would never know what had hit him.

"Dad, Jarod, please..." Sandy murmured.

They both ignored her, though neither of them spoke at first. Dan moved into the living room, arms crossed over his chest, and Sandy could see that her father was surprised—stunned—that after everything that had happened Jarod still had the nerve to behave this way.

"Sir!" Jarod snapped.

"What?" Dan demanded.

"How could you?"

"How could I what?"

"You—you—seducer! I asked you—I begged you!—I—"

"Jarod, what are you talking about?"

"I just hope that you intend to do something. Something honorable. You promised me, you know. When I came to ask you—"

"Damn it, Jarod—"

"I should really punch you right in the nose."

"Jarod!" Sandy screamed, really alarmed.

"You're the one with the experience! You're the one who played around. You knew what you were doing! And she didn't! I told you that! How could you? How could you have behaved with such a total lack of responsibility?"

Dan stared at Jarod blankly. What in God's name...? "Jarod, what are you talking about?"

"She's pregnant!" Jarod exploded. And then he started to laugh, as if it had just struck him how funny—how pathetically funny—the entire situation was. "My mother, Mr. Marquette, is pregnant."

Dan inhaled sharply. She couldn't be. Well, she could be, but if she was, she couldn't know already. Could she? Well, maybe. They had all those newfangled things out on the market—you could know almost anything right away.

It felt as if something exploded in his head, and then in his heart. A cascade of stars and gunpowder, emotion so fierce that he could barely endure it.

What was she thinking?

He started to wonder just how long she had known, and why he had to hear this from Jarod and why—why the hell she hadn't come to him!

"Sir! Did you hear me?"

Dan blinked. Jarod was still standing there, staring at him. There was suddenly a softening in that belligerent young face.

"Don't you see, sir? Can't you understand why I was so upset? Mom is as innocent as a babe in the woods, and you've been dating for almost twenty years! I was afraid of something like this. Well, not really. Not at first. I was afraid she would fall in love with you, and then you would leave her. But now...well, now you just have to make your intentions real clear to me. My mother is pregnant, expecting your child, and I want to know just what you intend to do about it."

It was a logical question, Dan decided. But it seemed so damn strange, Jarod standing there staring at him in outrage. Telling him that Kelly was pregnant.

Kelly was pregnant.

His daughter was pregnant, and now Kelly was, too. He didn't think there could be this much procreation going on if he'd decided to raise jackrabbits for a living.

"My God," he murmured.

"Dad?" Sandy said.

"Are you sure?" Dan suddenly asked Jarod.

"Well, I think so."

"Your mother told you?"

"Ah . . . no."

"Dad needs a chair, I think."

"He needs a drink, *I* think."

"I'll get him one."

Sandy ran off. Dan kept staring at Jarod, shaking his head slightly. "How can she know? How can she be sure?"

Jarod smiled at him crookedly. "I'm not supposed to know, but I saw her, uh, test."

Dan nodded vaguely. Kelly was pregnant.

Kelly wasn't speaking to him.

He smiled slowly, ruefully. Did that really matter? Nothing in life was ever going to be perfect. He had a temper, she had a temper, and they were different people. They hadn't met under the best of circumstances.

Kelly was pregnant. . . .

They were going to have a child. It would be nice to have a boy. He'd loved having a daughter. Another daughter would be fine, too. He just wanted a healthy baby, the same way he had just wanted Sandy to be a healthy baby. But . . .

A boy would be nice. Of course, in a way, he already had his boy. He had Jarod. This wise-talking stud here—Kelly's son. Dan had had a beautiful daughter, and he'd raised her to be sweet and smart and only a little bit foolish when it came to falling in love. But even in that, she'd had some sense—she'd fallen in love with Jarod McGraw. And even though Dan had been mad enough to want to punch the kid a few times, his priorities were in the right place. He knew something about responsibility; he loved Sandy.

He loved his mother.

"Dad, here's a Scotch."

"Sir, just what do you intend to do?"

"Oh, Jarod! I can't believe it!" Sandy laughed suddenly. "Is she really going to have a baby? I love it!"

Dan swallowed the Scotch. He had to see her. He had to tell Kelly herself—not Jarod—that he loved her. That he wanted to stand by her, that he was thrilled, that he wanted to marry her and raise their child together.

"Sir!"

"I love your mother, Jarod," Dan said quietly. He walked across the room to set his Scotch down on a table. "I've got to go see her."

"Oh!" Jarod said suddenly. "No. Uh, no, you can't do that."

"What do you mean, I can't do that?" Dan demanded darkly. "You've just told me—"

"Yes, I know, but I wasn't supposed to."

"Jarod, you didn't just come in here talking, you came in swinging and demanding—"

"I know! I know! But I promised Mom that I wouldn't mention her name. I, uh, I just had to know what you were feeling and what you were thinking.

But she's ready to disown me as it is. You can't let her know I told you."

There was silence for a moment, a silence in which Jarod stared at Dan.

"Dad?" Sandy said softly. "Shouldn't you let her come to you?"

"Yeah, yeah, maybe I should," Dan muttered.

He picked his Scotch back up and drank the remainder in a single swallow. He glanced at his watch. "She should be here by now!"

"Dad," Sandy protested, "give Kelly a chance."

"Yeah, yeah, I guess I should."

He started to pace the room. Jarod and Sandy sat together on the couch, their fingers entwined.

"How much of a chance?" Dan suddenly exploded.

Sandy inclined her head, reflecting on the question. "A few days, maybe. A week—"

"A week!" Dan thundered.

Jarod stood up uneasily. "Sandy, I'm not so sure that Dan should wait." He swallowed. "I wasn't supposed to tell you, but I did, and I guess she has a right to know. I mean, well, I only did it because I love her. But, uh, I'm..."

"What?" Dan demanded.

"I'm a little bit worried. About what she might decide to do."

"To do?" Dan's voice became sharper and his eyes narrowed dangerously.

"She might be thinking about, well, about not having the baby," Jarod said in a long rush. "That's why I had to tell you. Before she could do something like that. You can't let her. You can't. You have to stop her.''

Dan stared at Jarod for a long minute, then he reached for his jacket and started with long, furious strides for the door.

"Damn right, I do. Damn right."

Chapter 13

Dan was relieved to see Kelly's car in her driveway. He parked haphazardly on the lawn, slammed his door and hurried up the walk, only to discover the front door opening as he reached it.

"Where do you think you're going?"

He hadn't meant to shout, but it had taken him aback to see that she was going out. She was wearing a fawn skirt with a slit in the back, a soft-beige blouse, a tweed jacket, stockings and heels. High heels, the kind she never failed to wear when she wanted to feel mature—and tall.

She was also wearing a little hat, and though she quickly cast him a gaze of dismay, when she lowered her head, he could no longer see her eyes, no longer read the emotion within them.

"Kelly, where do you think you're going?"

It was more of a growl this time, but he hadn't meant that, either.

"Dan!" she murmured, looking up again. Dan smiled a little grimly, because he was certain that she was trying to determine whether or not he knew—whether Jarod had betrayed her to him.

"One more time, Kelly." He blocked the doorway, hands on his hips. "Where are you going?"

"Out." she told him boldly.

"Get back in the house."

When she didn't move, he glared at her and asked, "Where do you think you're going?"

"The grocery store."

"The hell you are!"

"I am!"

"We're going to talk about it."

Her blue eyes widened incredulously. "We're going to talk about the grocery store?"

"You're not headed for any grocery store! Not dressed like that!" He took her shoulders and steered her back into the house, following closely in her wake, then closing the door behind them with his foot.

"What do you think you're doing?" she demanded heatedly.

"You're not leaving! We're going to talk!"

She was silent for a minute, then said coldly, "Do you know, that's one of your major problems."

"What's one of my major problems?"

"That temper of yours! It's awful. It's ridiculous that you think you can just boss everyone around. Every time you get mad, you get abusive—"

"I'm never abusive!"

"The first time I met you, you were yelling. And the next thing I knew, you were yelling at me again, because my son and your daughter chose my cabin in which to... to..."

"Damn it, Kelly, I'm sorry! I know I had no right to lay that one on you, and I apologize."

"Then you nearly attacked my son!" Kelly said, outraged.

"The hell I did!" Dan protested furiously. "I didn't touch the little brat—and he *was* being a brat, Kelly. You know," he said thoughtfully, "that's part of your problem."

"My problem?"

"That's right, lady. Princess of Fantasy. Jarod was wrong, and you knew it. But you had to protect your child, protect him all the way. Well, Kelly, he isn't a kid anymore, and you'd better realize that. He has to be responsible for his own actions."

Her fingers twisted around the strap of her purse. "Jarod is a good human being, Dan Marquette, and don't you dare try to tell me differently—"

"I'm extremely fond of Jarod. He's a good kid, and so's Sandy. But I can't see rewarding either one of them for misbehaving."

"No, you would just go into one of your famous Dan Marquette tempers!"

"Kelly—"

"Dan, let me by!"

"Not on your life, Kelly."

"You can't do this! Get out of my way!"

"Kelly, we've got to talk."

"We just did."

"About us, not the kids."

She stared at him, then sighed with a great display of patience.

"Where were you going?" he asked calmly.

"To the grocery store! Oh, excuse me. If it's any of your business, I was also going to the art shop!"

Kelly, don't! he prayed silently. You talked about my temper and my tantrums and me thinking that I can bulldoze people into doing things my way. But don't you see, Kelly? You have all the power.

She smiled at him suddenly.

"Excuse me, Dan, will you? I'll be right back."

She headed for the kitchen, and, like a total dunce, he watched her go. It wasn't until he heard the door slam that he realized she intended to leave him standing there all the damn day—or at least until he got smart enough to realize that she had left by the back.

"Kelly!"

In a fury he went racing after her. She had already reached the lawn.

He didn't handle things very well then.

But he couldn't think very clearly. Damn her! She hadn't even told him! Hadn't even seen fit to tell him the truth!

He went flying out to the lawn after her.

Flying right into her.

He tackled her, and they lay on the lawn together. For a minute she just stared up at him in dismay and surprise, and then she brought her fists crashing against him.

"Dan Marquette, get off me! Of all the nerve—"

"Kelly, we've got to talk."

"Dan, someone could see!"

"I don't give a damn, Kelly."

"They'll arrest you!" she warned him fiercely.

When he didn't answer, her fists started flying again. He caught her wrists and smiled. Of all the absurd times to see how beautiful she was! How small and fine and delicate and beautifully blond, with those immense eyes . . .

Those eyes were the killers. One look, and a man was lost. Forever.

"Dan, damn you—"

"I love you, Kelly!"

"Dan!"

She started to struggle again, and he stretched her hands high over her head, then leaned down and kissed her.

He held her there, loving her lips, thrusting his tongue deep into her mouth, feeling a rush of emotion wash through him, sweeping them both away.

They could have been on a deserted beach. On a mountain blanketed with spring greenery and soft flowers. They could have been anywhere, and it wouldn't have mattered.

She ceased to struggle, and her lips softened.

He told himself that she was in love with him. That she just didn't want to see it at the moment because she was afraid. Afraid to start over. Afraid to repeat what had happened before.

He drew away from her. She wasn't struggling anymore. She was panting slightly, her breasts rising and falling with the exertion. He was dying to touch them, except that he wasn't sure he wanted to go quite that far right there on her lawn. Her eyes were slightly glazed, her lips were still parted and damp, and she was staring at him, completely confused.

"I love you, Kelly," he said again.

"Dan, let me up—" she began, attempting to dislodge him.

"I want to marry you."

"Dan, what—"

"Don't do it, Kelly! I'm begging you!"

"Don't do what?"

"I love you. I love you so much. I want us to spend our lives together. Just—please—don't do it."

"Dan! What are you talking about?"

"Kelly..." He looked at her sadly. She was convinced that he had finally snapped.

"Dan...?"

He stood, taking her tenderly but forcefully into his arms. Then he walked back toward the house still carrying her.

"Dan!"

He opened the door, then slammed it behind them.

"Dan?"

"I love you, Kelly."

"What's going on, Dan?"

"Shut up, Kelly."

He was on the stairway by then.

"Jarod!" she exclaimed suddenly. "Why, that little brat!"

"Don't do it, Kelly, please don't."

"Okay, Dan. If it means that much to you, I won't go to the grocery store. Or to the art shop, either."

"Kelly, damn it! I'm talking about—"

"Dan! Stop!" She couldn't help smiling, even if a little sadly. "Dan, I don't know what Jarod said to you, but what you're thinking just isn't true."

He swallowed. "Kelly, he saw—"

"He saw a test, Dan. I—I was frightened. In fact, I was a little panicky. But I'm not pregnant. Honest."

"Oh."

He sat down, right on the stairway, with her in his arms.

"You—you wouldn't lie to me?"

"No." She smiled again and touched his lips with a light kiss. She really did adore him. Despite all the awful fights they managed to get into, she adored him. "Dan?"

"Hmm?"

"Dan, you seem..."

He kissed her back and looked at her sheepishly. "I—I'm disappointed."

"What?"

He nodded sheepishly. Then he held her close, rubbing his chin across her head gently. "I wanted it to be true. I wanted us to have a child. I want to marry you, Kelly. I want to live together, to be man and wife. I want all of it."

"Dan, that's lovely."

"It's what I feel. Kelly...?"

She stroked his cheek a little wonderingly, then rested her head against his shoulder. "Dan, I'm glad the kids love each other. And I'm happy for the years that I had with Jarod's father, but...sometime, sometime in my life, I wanted to fall in love, get married, and *then* have a child? Do you understand?"

He kissed her fingers. "But..."

"But what?"

"Kelly, I love you." He paused. "Did you think about it at all?"

She didn't pretend to misunderstand. "Okay, I did spend just a little bit of time thinking that we would have a beautiful baby."

"We could do it the way you want, you know."

"We could?"

"I'm in love with you."

"I love you, too."

"So marry me—and *then* we'll have a baby."

"Dan... maybe we should take more time."

"Maybe we should seize every moment that we can."

His arms tightened around her, and he stood, then started up the stairs.

"Dan..."

He laughed, plucked the little hat off her head and sent it flying. Her hair fell over his arms, all gold and soft and rich and lustrous.

"Dan, if you think that we're going to—"

"Make love," he said, smiling.

"We weren't speaking an hour ago."

They were at the door to her room by then.

"Dan!" Kelly protested. She was laughing, but she was serious even so. "You can't do this. Not now. The kids will be worried about us!"

"Let them worry!" He was grinning. Diabolical, devilish, rakish. Sensual and sexy, and she felt as if he was on fire. He laid her on the bed, then stripped off his shirt and kicked off his shoes. She was still staring at him.

"Dan..."

She started to rise, but he made a dive for the bed, pinned her to the mattress and kissed her.

The kiss seared through her. His kisses always had that power she thought. Hot and wet, his lips touched hers, making her feel electrical, magical. The kiss made her feel that she was on fire, too.

"Marry me, Kelly. Fly away with me."

"Dan..."

"Let me talk you into it."

He drew away from her. She didn't know that she was staring at him again, mesmerized, ridiculously hypnotized by his touch, until she realized that he was methodically taking off her shoes and dropping them to the floor. Then he slid his fingers along her thighs to find the tops of her stockings. Slowly, slowly, he slipped them from her legs, his kiss burning against her thigh where the material disappeared.

"Dan... you're not talking."

"I'm trying to be exceptionally eloquent."

Her jacket joined her shoes on the floor.

How could a man with such large hands manipulate tiny pearl buttons so easily? she wondered. Oh, he was good, he really was good.

She gasped sharply as sensations shot through her, warm and stirring and exciting. Those same agile fingers had found the hook of her bra and released it.

Then his mouth fastened over her breast, over her nipple, maneuvering, manipulating, teeth grazing, sucking in...

It hurt. The pleasure was so great that it actually hurt. Heat poured through her body and gathered between her legs, and she was suddenly forced to cry out his name and wrap her arms around him. Her skirt had somehow gotten hiked up around her hips, and his fingers suddenly lost their agility when they reached her panties. She heard them rip, but she didn't care. She remembered that they were supposed to be discussing something, and her fingers wound tightly into his hair, and she dragged him up, forcing him to look at her.

"Oh, Dan, I want you. So much."

"Good," he murmured grimly. "Now all I have to do is make you want me forever and ever." He caught her hand and brought it against him. Against his belt and his jeans. She instinctively knew what he wanted, and she complied. She felt a wonderful shiver and then a cascade of desire and longing as he moved, hard and strong and demanding, at her touch.

A ragged sound escaped him, and he buried his head against her throat, his fingers moving tenderly, achingly into her hair.

"Kelly... marry me."

"Are you bribing me, or threatening me?"

"Begging, at this point! Well...?"

His whisper hung in the air, heavy with emotion and need, tense and heated and sweet.

She whispered his name. His weight shifted as he moved her, and once again she looked up at him. She smiled suddenly and locked her fingers around his neck, then pulled herself up to him and pressed her lips against his.

And then she did everything else she had been longing to do. Stroked the length of his back. Stroked his chest and his hips. She whispered, and she listened to his whispers, and she gave soft cries of delight each time he touched her.

She felt him become one with her, and she ached for their loving to come to an end, because it felt so wonderful that it was close to pain. And then she prayed that it would never end, because nothing had ever been so good. She rose and she fell, and she rose again....

And when the end really came, it was explosive and volatile and wonderful, and even when she reached the crest she was in awe, disbelieving, afraid to believe....

Afraid to believe that it could really be for a lifetime. That love as well as children could be real. Forever.

But she couldn't let herself drift along; she couldn't just savor the day and the afterglow and the damp heat of his body, so protectively and tenderly stretched beside her.

She ran her fingers through the mat of hair on his chest, keeping her head lowered against his collarbone.

He shifted, forcing her beneath him, and stared deeply into her eyes. "Kelly, I love you. I want to marry you."

She looked at him, gnawing her lower lip. "Dan, I swear to you—I am not pregnant."

"I believe you. The point is that I love you. And you love me. I want to get married—and I do want a baby. If you want one, too, that is. Whenever you want."

"Soon. I'm not getting any younger."

"Then..."

He clutched her hand and kissed it. The back, and then the palm—and then her fingers, one by one. "Does that mean you'll marry me?"

"Oh. Oh, Dan!"

He was suddenly the one on the bottom; she was straddled on top of him, planting delighted kisses all over his face.

"Kelly—"

"Dan, I love you. I do. Your temper is obnoxious, of course, but I do love you!"

He struggled and managed to rise up on his elbows to challenge her eyes. "Does that mean that you'll marry me?"

"Yes."

"Really?"

"Yes! Yes!"

"Kelly!"

They changed positions again. "Kelly, I love you. I love you. I love you...."

"What's wrong?" she asked when he paused.

"Listen!"

And then she heard it, too. A car pulling into the driveway.

Kelly stared at Dan in alarm, then pushed him away with a tremendous shove and raced to the window.

"It's them!"

"The kids?"

"Yes! Get dressed!"

"I will."

"Now! Hurry!"

Kelly was already struggling back into her clothes, but Dan simply refused to be rushed. He buttoned his shirt slowly while Kelly cast him a scathing look.

"Dan, they'll know what we've been up to!"

"Maybe."

"Then—"

"Don't worry, Kelly. I've had it with interference. I'll handle this. I promise."

"What am I worried about?" she murmured suddenly. "That little rat of a son of mine went crawling over to your house to tell tales that weren't even true!"

"Hey! That little rat and his misconstrued information got us speaking again."

He was only half-dressed, but he took the time to drag Kelly back to him, kissing her quickly. "I'll handle them," he promised.

She was doubtful, but she bit back a reply, because she was convinced that the more she said, the slower he would be.

She raced for the door, then raced back to brush her hair. There was nothing like totally messed-up hair for a dead giveaway.

She shot Dan one more quick glance and started for the stairway. The kids weren't in the living room. She could have sworn that she smelled something cooking in the kitchen, so she headed that way.

Sandy was standing at the stove, while Jarod was setting the table, for four. He glanced up at her. "Drink, Mom?"

Sandy gazed at him quickly. "She really shouldn't, Jarod."

"One beer will be okay."

Kelly crossed her arms over her chest, watching the two of them. "Oh, really... son?"

He grinned and brought her a beer. "One." He kept smiling, looking behind her, and she realized that Dan was standing there. "Beer, sir?"

"Sure," Dan drawled easily. Kelly was aware that he was watching Jarod with both suspicion and fond amusement.

"We're having Sandy's special fried shrimp and a big salad for dinner," Jarod said. "It was the best we could do so quickly. Sit down, please."

Dan and Kelly exchanged glances and shrugged, then obediently slid into seats across from each other.

Sandy turned around holding a big plate of shrimp. "Now the first thing is that the two of you have to realize that you have options. Kelly, I love you to death, and you know that."

"And she wants you to have the baby, Mom. She really does."

"Of course," Sandy agreed. "It's just that it is your life. You have to live it, not Jarod or me."

"We'll help you, of course," Jarod said barely suppressing a smile. "We'll do everything we can for you."

"That's very nice of you," Dan said dryly. Then he looked at Kelly, and they both burst into laughter. Kelly sat back and took a bite of Sandy's shrimp. It was delicious. Jarod was going to eat well, she decided—probably better than Dan!

She walked around the table and kissed Sandy, then hugged and kissed Jarod. Then she went over to stand behind Dan.

"Thank you. Both of you," she said. "You darling little wiseacres. But we're not having a baby."

"Mother, you didn't—"

"No, I didn't. I never was. I told you that."

"But—but—you acted so suspiciously!"

"You really shouldn't spread tales."

Dan stood beside Kelly. He slipped his hands around her waist, and she laced her fingers through his as he spoke. "We've decided, though, that we are going to make a baby. Or spend some time trying," he said conversationally.

"Dad!" Sandy gasped.

"You see, I love Kelly, and she loves me."

"Very much," Kelly tossed in.

"And we're going to get married."

"Oh!" Sandy cried. Then she burst into tears and raced around the table to hug Kelly, and then her father.

Jarod didn't cry, but he did lift his mother off the ground and whirl her around. He started to give Dan a manly handshake, but then he gave his almost-father-in-law a big hug, too.

Finally Sandy said, "Oh! Dinner is going to be ice-cold."

Dan glanced at his watch and shrugged, then smiled pleasantly at Kelly. "I guess we have time."

She didn't have the faintest idea what he was talking about, but she decided to take her cue from him. She sat down and, with a very straight face, began to eat her salad.

Sandy and Jarod stared at them in obvious confusion.

"Time?" Jarod asked.

"Kelly and I kind of have a date," Dan said idly, tasting a shrimp. "Sandy, this really is delicious. Wonderful. Jarod, did you finally decide on Georgetown? You two have to get all the paperwork in, you know."

"Yes, Dad," Sandy answered for Jarod. "We both decided on Georgetown. For now. I'm not going to start until January—"

"Sandy..." Dan frowned.

"I promise! I really will start in January."

"She will, sir, I guarantee it. It's just that the baby will be so small that first semester."

Dan gazed at Kelly, who shrugged. "It seems like a sound plan to me. Jarod will have to start in the fall, or he'll lose his athletic scholarship."

Dan nodded. "Are you about done, Kelly?"

"Yes." She still didn't have the faintest idea what he was up to.

"Where are you going?" Jarod demanded.

"Off to the islands," Dan said. He winked at Kelly and finished his beer in a quick swallow. He grinned at the kids. "We're flying down to the Bahamas to get married. We'll be gone for a week."

"What?"

Kelly gasped the question along with her son, who was on his feet, staring at them with amazement.

"Now? Right away?" Kelly asked, dazed.

Dan pulled her close and smiled. "I think it's a wonderful idea, don't you?"

She smiled slowly in return. Marvelous. They'd be married. Man and wife. Living together. "I think it's divine."

"Oh, wow, maybe Sandy and I should come, too."

"Not on your life!" Dan told him.

"But—"

"Sorry, Jarod. You and Sandy are getting married in church in June, just like we planned, with a reception and a guest list and a nine-yard-long train."

"But—"

"You see, Kelly and I are older than you two." He arched a brow at Kelly, and his smile was the most diabolical she had seen yet. "We can do things like just run off to the Bahamas if we want. We've already graduated from high school."

"Yeah, but—"

"Sorry, Jarod. Really. The two of you are just going to have to wait."

"Wait—and behave!" Kelly added sternly.

"Oh, they'll behave."

Kelly grinned. Jarod and Sandy had just exchanged very open glances. Glances that said, while the cats were away, the mice could play.

"Reeves will be expecting you both in about..." Dan paused to glance at his watch again. "In about thirty minutes."

Kelly gazed skeptically at Dan, who leaned down to whisper to her. "I called from your bedroom phone. He knows exactly what we're doing, and he'll keep his eye on them."

Kelly couldn't help but grin in return. "I'll just run up and pack a few things."

"Not too many! We can buy whatever we need. Ah, yes!" He sat down again and settled back in his chair, smiling at the kids. "Sun, sand, tennis, sailing..."

"Not fair!" Sandy pouted.

Dan just laughed. But then he stood again and kissed his daughter warmly on the cheek.

"Your time will come, baby. Honest. And you'll have a beautiful wedding to remember all your lives."

A few minutes later Kelly was back downstairs. Kisses and hugs flowed between the four of them again. Kisses and hugs—and reminders that homework had to be done.

And then they were outside and headed for the airport, and Kelly still wasn't terribly sure that she could believe the whole thing.

"Was—was Reeves upset?" she asked Dan.

"Oh, no. Nothing really surprises or upsets Reeves. He's a little... confused, though."

"Oh? Why?"

"He says that he was used to being a gentleman's gentleman, and that it's bad enough that he's going to be a nanny, but on top of that, he's not quite sure whose nanny he's supposed to be!"

Kelly started to laugh. "Well, since we don't have a baby yet..." She reached over and entwined her fingers with Dan's, then leaned happily against his shoulder.

"We will," he promised her.

"I love you so much."

"Mrs. Kelly Marquette. I love the sound of it."

"Umm. I adore it."

She closed her eyes happily. She had been given a real second chance at happiness. It didn't happen often, not even in fantasy.

"We'll just have to loan him to the kids, that's all," she said with a sigh.

"What?"

"Reeves. We will need him! Hey, I didn't get to be old and mature for nothing! If and when we have our baby, I want to enjoy it. I want Reeves to help with the house and the food and—life! So that I can really enjoy this baby while it's little. But..." She smiled sheepishly at Dan, then leaned contentedly against his shoulder once again. "I love our big babies, too. When Sandy has her baby, I'm sure Reeves won't mind staying with them for a while."

"Sounds generous," Dan teased.

"Oh, not really." Kelly kissed his fingers. "Because I'll have you, Mr. Marquette."

"Mr. and Mrs. Marquette."

"All alone."

"Together."

Epilogue

She had been standing by the fence watching him for a long time. Well, maybe not so long, but it felt like forever.

Watching everything about him. His hands on the ball. His smile. His hair, catching in the breeze. His eyes, when he glanced her way. His midriff, sleek and taut beneath the tattered edge of his sweatshirt.

Kelly had come to watch him quite specifically. Of course, she couldn't possibly have missed him. He was six-foot-three—a standout in any crowd. Striking, handsome—young, she thought with pride. He was absolutely beautiful.

Yet none of those superficial things was what had drawn her. Not from the beginning, and not now. It had been his smile, and his passion, and all the things inside him. Oh, he was far from perfect. He was temperamental, with his ego and his stubborn streak and his impatience. But he was always able to step back in the end; he saw his mistakes, and he was always quick to apologize. He didn't promise to be perfect in the future, because, of course, no one could. But she knew that always, through thick and thin, they could talk, and he would always be there for her.

It had begun the first time she saw him: love at first sight. And that love had deepened and broadened and grown with every step they took together.

Now she felt anxious, and her fingers curled into the fencing. She willed him to look her way, and at last he did.

She smiled.

He stood still, tossing the football up in the air, then catching it. At last he came toward her.

He stood by the fence, and they were just inches apart. She was in love. Head over heels in love. She felt as if she would never love again as she did at the moment.

"Hi," she said, emotion making her almost shy.

"Hi."

"Want to go for a ride?"

"Yeah."

"I love you."

"I love you...." His voice trailed away, his heart catching at the sight of her smile. "You're the most beautiful creature ever to walk this earth. A fantasy creation yourself..."

She laughed, a husky sound that caught in her throat. Warmth raced through her. She was breathless, barely able to speak in return.

"You're a liar. I look like a blimp! But I...oh, I love you. I love you, and I need you, and I want you...."

It wasn't meant to seduce; it wasn't even meant to be sexy. They were honest words, meant for a lifetime.

The breeze picked up, and a shadow, rich with dark warmth and promise, fell over the valley. He dropped the football, and his fingers curled over hers where they clung to the fence.

Finally he let go of her hand and walked through the gate to stand in front of her. A slow smile lit his face, and he raised his hand, palm flat, toward her. She put her own hand against his, and he watched her eyes as their fingers entwined.

"Do you have your car?" he asked her.

"Yes. Where do you want to go?"

"I know this wonderful place. It's a cabin, up in the hills."

She laughed, and they linked arms as they walked toward the car. In no time at all, it seemed, they were at the cabin.

While it was still light they wandered down to the stream, where they wound up laughing and showering each other with the cold mountain water. Naturally he built a fire as soon as they went back inside.

As they sat beside it, he touched her cheek, and in the gentle fire light they gazed into each other's eyes. Finally their clothes were shed.

He'd never seen anyone more beautiful. She had wonderful hair, and it seemed to be a part of the fire, cascading in lustrous curls over her breasts, glowing against the ivory of her flesh. Her breasts were beautiful and perfect and full, and when he looked at her, he could barely speak. Yet when she was in his arms he did, telling her how much he loved her. Each time he touched her body he murmured of her beauty, and she laughed, and then he told her that it was true: she was more beautiful than ever.

Finally their laughter faded. Love led the way for her, a gentle, tender path to ecstasy, sweet and torrid. She felt dazzled, as if he were the sun and the air and the earth all in one.

She belonged to him, with all her heart.

No one had ever loved so well. And no one had ever made love as they did. So deeply, so completely. Heart and body and soul . . .

Love.

He wanted to run out of the cabin, stark naked. She made him feel so male and strong and wonderful. He wanted to proclaim to the world that she was his, his beloved, his forever.

She lay with her cheek against his chest, his fingers wound into her hair, and together they watched the flames playing softly in the hearth.

"Sometimes I still can't believe it," she murmured suddenly, turning to stare down at him.

"Believe what?"

"How happy we are. From such a beginning! All of us, really."

He held her face tenderly between his hands and looked at her with a rueful grin. "Sometimes, just sometimes, life can be just a little like a fantasy. There can be magic. We've found that magic. At least, I have. It's in your eyes."

"Oh, that's so nice."

He grinned again. "Yes, I thought so. Rather good for a grim old historian, don't you think?"

"Humph!" She would have said more, but the phone started ringing. They looked at each other with surprise, because no one should have known where they were.

Jarod. Of course! Jarod had seen them leave, and he must have guessed where they were going. Except that he wouldn't have interrupted them—unless . . .

"Sandy!" they exclaimed simultaneously, staring wide-eyed at each other and jumping up, then colliding in their efforts to reach the phone.

Dan won the race, but he held the receiver away from his ear so they both could hear.

"Dan?"

"Jarod?"

"It's a boy!"

"A boy! It's a boy!" Dan repeated for Kelly.

"I heard!"

"Eight pounds, two ounces."

"Congratulations! We'll be right there."

"Good." Jarod hesitated just a second. "Put your clothes on first, will you, please?"

Kelly grabbed the phone from Dan. "I heard that, young man!"

"Sorry! Get here quickly. Mom, he's beautiful!"

"Of course he's beautiful. He's my grandchild!"

She dropped the receiver and stared at her husband. "Oh, Dan! It's true! We're grandparents."

He kissed her lips quickly. "Yes, it's true." He drew her against him. "And," he whispered very softly to her, "thank God for those darling little procreationists! We might never have met without them."

"Never loved."

"Never married."

She was able to smile up at him at last. "Let's go see the baby."

"Only if you calm down. Ours isn't due for another two months, and I'd like it to wait until then."

She made a face at him. "I *am* calm. Oh! My God! We're grandparents!"

"I'll go see that baby without you, Kelly," he teased.

"You will not!"

She smiled sweetly, showing him how calm she was, while he helped her back into her clothes.

"Actually," he told her, "you do look like a blimp."

"You wouldn't dare say that if I weren't a grandparent!" she said reproachfully.

He laughed and told her that she was the most beautiful grandmother he had ever seen, and the sexiest. "Definitely the most beautiful pregnant grandmother ever," he assured her.

And so, naturally, being sophisticated and mature this time around, she stuck out her tongue at him and preceded him out the door.

* * * * *

Don't miss these other titles by
New York Times bestselling author

HEATHER GRAHAM POZZESSERE!

Silhouette Intimate Moments®

#07416	HATFIELD AND McCOY	$3.29 ☐
#07525	THE TROUBLE WITH ANDREW	$3.50 ☐

Silhouette Shadows®

#27001	THE LAST CAVALIER	$3.50 ☐

Best of the Best

#48279	DOUBLE ENTENDRE	$4.50 ☐
#48280	THE GAME OF LOVE	$4.50 U.S. ☐
		$4.99 CAN. ☐

By Request

#20106	BRAVE HEARTS	$5.50 U.S. ☐
		$5.99 CAN. ☐

TOTAL AMOUNT	$
POSTAGE & HANDLING	$
($1.00 for one book, 50¢ for each additional)	
APPLICABLE TAXES*	$_____
TOTAL PAYABLE	$_____
(check or money order—please do not send cash)	

To order, complete this form and send it, along with a check or money order
for the total above, payable to Silhouette Books, to: **In the U.S.:** 3010 Walden
Avenue, P.O. Box 9077, Buffalo, NY 14269-9077; **In Canada:** P.O. Box 636,
Fort Erie, Ontario, L2A 5X3.

Name: _____

Address: _____ City: _____

State/Prov.: _____ Zip/Postal Code: _____

*New York residents remit applicable sales taxes.
Canadian residents remit applicable GST and provincial taxes.   SHGPBACK4

Silhouette®
TM

Take 3 of
"The Best of the Best™"
Novels FREE
Plus get a FREE surprise gift!

Special Limited-time Offer
Mail to The Best of the Best™

> 3010 Walden Avenue
> P.O. Box 1867
> Buffalo, N.Y. 14269-1867

YES! Please send me 3 free novels and my free surprise gift. Then send me 3 of "The Best of the Best™" novels each month. I'll receive the best books by the world's hottest romance authors. Bill me at the low price of $3.74 each plus 25¢ delivery and applicable sales tax, if any.* That's the complete price and a savings of over 10% off the cover prices—quite a bargain! I understand that accepting the books and gift places me under no obligation ever to buy any books. I can always return a shipment and cancel at any time. Even if I never buy another book from Harlequin, the 3 free books and the surprise gift are mine to keep forever.

183 BPA ANV9

Name	(PLEASE PRINT)	
Address	Apt. No.	
City	State	Zip

This offer is limited to one order per household and not valid to current subscribers.
*Terms and prices are subject to change without notice. Sales tax applicable in N.Y.
All orders subject to approval.

UBOB-295 ©1990 Harlequin Enterprises Limited

The Loop™

Is the future what it's cracked up to be?

This June be careful what you wish for…because it could come true!

GETTING CONNECTED: ROBIN
by Coleen E. Booth

Robin Alston had had it! Ever since her mom died, she'd been playing maid for her dad and brother. It was time to let them wash their own laundry—if they could ever figure out how to use the washing machine. So she got a great apartment in a way better part of town and began dating a man who faced the tough issues head-on. But it wasn't long before Robin realized that getting out didn't always mean things would be getting better.…

The ups and downs of life as you know it continue with

GETTING HITCHED: CJ
by Wendy Corsi Staub (July)

Get smart. Get into "The Loop!"

Montana Mavericks™

Stories that capture living and loving
beneath the Big Sky, where legends live
on...and mystery lingers.

This June, find out why secrets never stay secret in

MAN WITH A PAST
by Celeste Hamilton

Some folks in Whitehorn talked her ear off and
some squirmed at the sight of her. But when reporter
Elizabeth Monroe got only a long, hard glare from
Jonas Bishop, she knew the man was hiding something.
Something every bit as scandalous as all the town's juicy
little secrets. Problem was, Jonas aroused much more
than just Elizabeth's suspicions....

Don't miss the exciting conclusion of the mystery with:

COWBOY COP
by Rachel Lee (July)

Only from _Silhouette_® where passion lives.

This July, bestselling author
Diana Palmer
reunites you with three more
legendary cowboys in

The Legend continues...

Three complete novels by one of your favorite
authors—all in one special collection!

SUTTON'S WAY
ETHAN
CONNAL

Together with Diana Palmer, these three rugged
Texans are sure to lasso your heart!

Available wherever *Silhouette*®

books are sold.

In June, get ready for thrilling romances and FREE BOOKS—Western-style— with...

WESTERN *Lovers*

You can receive the first 2 Western Lovers titles FREE!

June 1995 brings Harlequin and Silhouette's WESTERN LOVERS series, which combines larger-than-life love stories set in the American West! And WESTERN LOVERS brings you stories with your favorite themes... "Ranch Rogues," "Hitched In Haste," "Ranchin' Dads," "Reunited Hearts" the packaging on each book highlights the popular theme found in each WESTERN LOVERS story!

And in June, when you buy either of the Men Made In America titles, you will receive a WESTERN LOVERS title absolutely FREE! Look for these fabulous combinations:

♦ Buy ALL IN THE FAMILY
  by Heather Graham Pozzessere (Men Made In America) and receive a FREE copy of
  BETRAYED BY LOVE by Diana Palmer
  (Western Lovers)

♦ Buy THE WAITING GAME
  by Jayne Ann Krentz (Men Made In America) and receive a FREE copy of
  IN A CLASS BY HIMSELF by JoAnn Ross
  (Western Lovers)

Look for the special, extra-value shrink-wrapped packages at your favorite retail outlet!

HARLEQUIN® *Silhouette*®

Announcing
the New Pages & Privileges™ Program
from Harlequin® and Silhouette®

Get All This FREE
With Just One Proof-of-Purchase!

- **FREE Hotel Discounts** of up to 60% off at leading hotels in the U.S., Canada and Europe

- **FREE Travel Service** with the guaranteed lowest available airfares plus 5% cash back on every ticket

- **FREE $25 Travel Voucher** to use on any ticket on any airline booked through our Travel Service

- **FREE Petite Parfumerie** collection (a $50 Retail value)

- **FREE Insider Tips Letter** full of fascinating information and hot sneak previews of upcoming books

- **FREE Mystery Gift** (if you enroll before June 15/95)

And there are more great gifts and benefits to come!
Enroll today and become Privileged!
(see insert for details)

PROOF-OF-PURCHASE

Offer expires October 31, 1996

MMIA-PP2